$\mathcal{I}$ couldn't see into the hallway from the stairs, but I'd perfected a swing-around. I grabbed the end of the banister for momentum and swung into the hallway—

Bam!

I slammed right into a big, muscular Jason! He staggered forward and I crashed to the floor.

"Dani!" Tiffany said in a tone that clearly implied, "Are you an idiot or what?"

"You okay?" Jason asked.

And time stopped. Just like that. I'd promised Mom I'd have no interest whatsoever in Jason, but I could see now that I'd made a vow that was easier said than done. Who would have thought he'd be *this* hot?

ALSO BY RACHEL HAWTHORNE

Caribbean Cruising

Island Girls (and Boys)

Love on the Lifts

Thrill Ride

The Boyfriend League

RACHEL HAWTHORNE

HARPER TEEN

An Imprint of HarperCollins *Publishers*

HarperTeen is an imprint of HarperCollins
Publishers.

Library of Congress Catalog Card Number:
2006933594
ISBN-10: 0-06-113837-1
ISBN-13: 978-0-06-113837-9

Typography by Andrea Vandergrift

❖

First HarperTeen edition, 2007

For Alan,
my source for all things baseball.
Thanks, Big Guy.
On my personal roster, you're a 10.

Ragland Rattlers Team Roster

No.	Name	Position	Hottie Score
12	Gabe Alvarado	Pitcher	
50	Alan Beaubien	3B	10
22	Brandon Bentley	1B	10
24	Tom Blum	Outfielder	
7	Brad Cone	Shortstop	
11	Jason Davis	Pitcher	~~6~~ 10.5
10	Ethan Haracz	Outfielder	
14	Dean Hilker	1B	
20	Todd "Mac" McPherson	Catcher	9.5
31	Chase Parker	Shortstop	
19	Christopher Parsons	Outfielder	
4	Sean Peterson	3B	
3	Tyler Rayburn	2B	
2	Alex Roman	Outfielder	
27	Nate Wylan	Outfielder	

Chapter 1

Families Needed to Provide Homes for Rattlers

For anyone not familiar with Ragland, Texas, the front-page headline in that morning's *Ragland Tribune* may have seemed odd. But I'd lived in Ragland since the day I was born. I couldn't think of anything more exciting than living with a Rattler.

It was Thursday morning, and I'd grabbed the newspaper to check out my weekly column, "Runyon's Sideline Review," because it was always a rush to see my byline. But as I sat at the breakfast table, before I'd turned to the sports section where my column usually appeared, the headline had snagged my attention and the possibilities bombarded me.

I absolutely couldn't believe I hadn't thought of it before. Having a Rattler in the house would be awesome!

Okay, I don't mean the slithering-along-the-ground-tail-rattling-in-ominous-warning rattler. I mean the sexy, hot, to-die-for players on our town's collegiate baseball team. As part of the Lonestar League, the Ragland Rattlers was one of nine city teams in the north Texas area made up of college players who wanted to play baseball during the summer. Local families hosted the team players.

Apparently this year, they were a few families short. And what better family than mine?

I heard a car honk and knew it was my ride to the softball field. My best friend and I both played on the high school softball team, but during the summer we just played whenever we had time to arrange a game with friends, which wasn't very often. Between attending the major- and minor-league games played in the area, plus being almost-groupies to the collegiate league, we didn't have a lot of time to commit to organized sports of our own.

I mean, if the choice was playing on a field with girls or watching a field of guys, Bird and I were going to choose the guys every time.

Her real name is Barbara Sawyer, but when she was a baby, her dad had thought she looked like a tiny bird, always chirping for food, and so he started calling her Birdie, which, over time, became Bird. Sometimes you gotta wonder what parents are thinking when they name or nickname their kids.

My own dad, I knew exactly what he'd been thinking when I was born. He wanted a boy. Instead he got me. Definitely a girl.

A year before I came along, my mom had given him another daughter, Tiffany, and Mom figured two kids were more than enough, especially since she wasn't a stay-at-home mom. We were a two-income family with a two-income lifestyle. Mom worked as a legal secretary in a prestigious Dallas law firm about thirty miles south of Ragland.

Anyway, Dad decided if he wasn't going to have a son, he could at least have a son-sounding name in the family. Hence, my parents named me Danielle, which of course got shortened to Dani.

But it all worked out. I love my dad, and we're really close. He always took me fishing, taught me to play baseball, and gave me loads of his time. He's a sports fanatic. Whenever he says, "Let's go out to eat," we know we'll be going to a sports bar to watch NASCAR, baseball, football, basketball, and golf simultaneously on the plasma TVs hanging throughout the place.

Connecting with my dad has always meant connecting with sports. Over time, I've gained an appreciation for all sports. In fact, I plan to major in journalism when I go off to college in another year. I want to be a sports announcer.

Bird, however, insists that my desire for a career in sports reporting has nothing to do with my love of sports. "It's your other love: guys. You want to know what really goes on in the locker room, and you want to get up close and personal with those towel-wrapped hotties."

Her theory is a lot closer to the truth than I like to admit, because it makes me seem less than noble in my pursuit of a higher education.

My sister has no love of sports, but she tolerates the sports bars because most have a nice salad selection, and she watches what she eats the way I watch *Lost*, searching for all the hidden clues, only she's searching for hidden calories.

Mom dotes on Tiffany, beautiful Tiffany, who's been named Miss Teen Ragland three years in a row and spends way too much time polishing her tiara.

Not that I'm jealous of Tiffany or anything, but sometimes, when so many guys are hanging around her and ignoring me, it's hard not to feel like the ugly duckling.

Bird honked again. She has her own car. I share one with Tiffany, but she'd already called it for the day. Actually, she'd called it pretty much for the entire summer, and since she had "obligations," I was used to her getting what she wanted. Especially guys. I basically carry a mop to clean up their drool whenever she's around.

Did I mention my sister is gorgeous? Gaggingly so.

I picked up my softball cap from the table, settled it on my head, and pulled my reddish-brown shoulder-length hair, which I was presently wearing in a ponytail, through the opening in the back. Tiffany has thick, lustrous, amazing hair that's more red than brown, but not red enough that anyone would call her Red. It's glorious.

While mine tends to just . . . hang. Which is the reason I usually wear it pulled back.

I grabbed my glove off the counter and headed out the door. It was the first official week of summer, the first week of no homework, no classes, no schedules, no bells. I was in heaven.

There are only two things I like as much as I like summer: baseball and boys.

Not necessarily in that order. But baseball has always been an important part of my life. Boys not nearly as much. I've never had a boyfriend, and I'm really starting to get bummed out by that fact. After all, next year I'll be a senior. As far as I'm concerned, it's long past time I had a boyfriend.

Oh, I've had a date now and then, but nothing long-term, nothing serious, nothing that's had my heart doing cartwheels inside my chest. Nothing that even hinted at any permanence.

I spotted the familiar white Grand Am waiting at the curb, idling, and sounding like it was shaking something loose beneath the hood. It's way older than I am, but I wasn't complaining. I was just grateful Bird could provide a ride.

I opened the car door, slid inside, and buckled up. "Did you see this morning's *Tribune*?"

Bird glanced in the rearview mirror before pulling out into the street. "Are you kidding? Mom took it for the Wed and Dead sections."

Bird's mom sells real estate. Newly married couples need places to live, newly dead people . . . well, their houses need to be sold, usually to the newly wed.

"Why? Did I miss something interesting?" Bird asked.

"They need extra families to host the Rattlers."

"And this concerns us because?"

"What is the one thing you want more than anything else?"

"You mean other than your autographed

· 7 ·

Babe Ruth baseball?"

In his youth, my granddad had watched Ruth play, and had gotten his autograph on a baseball. He'd given it to me the first time I hit a home run.

"Yeah, other than that," I said.

"A boyfriend."

I twisted around in my seat so I could look at her directly and accurately judge her reaction to what I was about to suggest. She so didn't look like a bird. Well, maybe she did a little. A ruffled bird. Her blond hair was cut really short with different layers, so even when she styled it, it didn't look styled. It sorta poked out here and there, which she said made it easy to care for, because no one knew if she'd taken the time to fix it or not. Which in her case was usually not.

That's one of the things I love about Bird. She's completely the opposite of my sister. If not for Bird, I would have grown up believing that spending three hours minimum in the bathroom in the morning was a common practice.

Unlike Tiffany, Bird and I aren't really into

spending a lot of time working to be beautiful, which might be one reason neither of us has a boyfriend.

Or, as it had occurred to me when I saw that morning's headline, it could all boil down to opportunity.

"How do you get a boyfriend?" I asked.

"If I knew that, I'd have one," Bird said.

"Hanging around guys. And where are there lots of guys during the summer?"

Bird pulled into the parking lot near the softball/baseball fields. She turned to me and arched a brow in question. She's one of the few people I know who actually have that whole Spock thing going and can make one eyebrow shoot way up. "Are you going somewhere with this?"

"There are lots of guys playing for the Ragland Rattlers," I explained. "It's a team of potential boyfriends."

"Not so far. Do we not traditionally hang out at the ball field during every practice and every game?"

"But we've always been no-name spectators. This year we could move into the realm of something more important. Let's talk our parents into letting us sponsor players for the summer. Then we'll hang out with them, and they'll hang out with the team. We'll have an *in* that we've never had. We'll be like ambassadors to Ragland, making them feel welcome, showing them around. Before we know it, instant summer boyfriend!"

"Don't the families usually have sons that the baseball players can be comfortable around?"

I shrugged. "Maybe because girls-only families never offered. Besides, the article said the team *needs* families, so we'd have a good chance of being selected even if we don't have brothers."

Like me, Bird has an older sister. Stephanie's a sophomore at a nearby university, with her own "stud-muffin" as she refers to him. She's always telling Bird not to worry about not having a boyfriend, because boyfriends aren't really worth having until you get to college, anyway. Until then, they're too immature. So, a college baseball player for the summer sounded like an ideal compromise. We could get a head start on the whole older, mature guy thing.

"I can't see my mom letting a guy live with us. She won't even let Steph's boyfriend stay over when he comes to town to visit," Bird said.

"We'd promise not to date them."

"I thought dating them was the whole point."

"No, the point is getting them to introduce us around."

"Why would they want to do that?"

"Because we'll know all the happening stuff."

"Have you forgotten we live in Ragland? There is nothing 'happening.'"

"There's lots going on. You just have to know where to search for it, and that's where we come in. We can serve as the chamber of commerce to the collegiate team. We could even arrange some outings."

"Like they have time for outings."

It *was* a pretty intense schedule, with four or five games a week, almost always at night.

"We'll figure something out. The first hurdle is getting the guys into our houses."

"And you don't think they'll be the *one*?"

"No way. With those guys, we'll be wearing blinders. I can't think of anything worse than my parents knowing about me and a boy. It would be too weird."

"What if our guys are hot?"

"Bird, these are college students. Do you really want to date the boy who sees you before you've applied your mascara?"

"Good point. Plus, I hang my bras in the bathroom to dry. Are you sure we want to do this? Having a guy living in the house has the potential to be embarrassing. What if he reveals our darkest secrets to the team?"

"We don't have dark secrets." Bird and I are pretty much what-you-see-is-what-you-get girls. Maybe we need to be more mysterious. I filed that thought away for later. "He's our connection to the team, and eventually to a boyfriend. That's all. He's not going to *be* the boyfriend."

"I guess it wouldn't hurt to give it a shot."

"You might want to curb your enthusiasm."

"Sorry. I just see the potential for disaster. We've never lived with guys before."

"Our dads."

"Like they count."

"We could set up a hotline. Your sister knows a lot about boys."

"Okay," she said. "Let's do it."

We knocked our knuckles together.

She wiggled her eyebrows at me. "You might even get to have a look into the locker room without becoming a sports reporter."

I grinned. "With any luck . . ."

Now all we had to do was convince our parents.

Chapter 2

"This would be the perfect place for a baseball player to live," I said during dinner that evening.

Mom had picked up Chinese food on her way home. Tiffany was the only one eating with chopsticks. She thought it was important to respect the customs of all nations, just in case she ever decided to enter the Miss Universe pageant.

My dad had been listening intently as I explained how the team was in need of host families. He always paid close attention to anything I said, because I was the one in the family most likely to talk sports.

He'd recently taken to shaving his head, because his hair had started thinning on top.

One day Tiffany had said, "Dad, what *are* you holding on to? Go for the Bruce Willis look."

Since Tiffany is the fashion expert, he'd taken her advice. Unfortunately Dad more closely resembles Lex Luthor than Bruce Willis, and I'm still missing what little hair he'd had on his head before he took a razor to it.

"He'll be here more than three days," Dad said.

Ah, Dad's three-day rule. Any relatives worth having as company know to limit their stay to three days. After that, they all get on his nerves.

"Well, yeah, but we're not related to him. I thought your rule only applied to family," I said.

"Honestly, I think he just applies it to your grandparents," Mom said from the other end of the table.

"I guess we have plenty of space," he said.

We have four bedrooms upstairs: mine, Tiffany's, the junk room, and the official guest bedroom. Mom and Dad's bedroom is on the first floor, near the back of the house.

"Plus we have a great backyard," I

reminded him. "Sports-guy heaven."

Our backyard has a home plate and pitcher's mound properly measured off, a basketball goal with a half court, and a six-hole miniature golf course—all designed and built by my dad, the owner of Backyard Mania, a company that makes big-time sports equipment in miniature for people who want more than a swimming pool in their backyard.

Before I hit my teen years, I'd spent many summer days riding around with my dad, serving as his "assistant," carrying his clipboard, giving my approval to the many projects he'd been hired to build. He even had a motto: "Every project comes with Dani's seal of approval."

The past few years, though, I'd outgrown wanting to be his assistant. And he was okay with that. He may have even been relieved. He probably gets a lot more work done, because he doesn't have to make numerous DQ stops to satisfy my ice-cream addiction.

"Have you really thought this through?" Tiffany asked. "We won't be able to walk around upstairs in our underwear."

Tiffany has a habit of not even wearing that much. She isn't exactly Miss Modesty. She says she's used to baring it all, because during beauty contests she often shares changing rooms with other girls, and so she's learned to be proud of her body and feel "comfortable with its natural state."

"I have a bathrobe," I said. "Or I could throw on shorts and a tank."

"I don't know," Mom said. "A boy in the house . . ." Her voice trailed off as though her thoughts were traveling into R-rated territory.

"It's not like we're going to date him, Mom. Worse than seeing Tiff without her clothes, he may see her without her makeup."

"No way!" Tiffany screeched. "I don't leave my room without makeup."

"Exactly. It would be kinda icky dating a guy who was living with us, who wouldn't always see us at our best. So, getting involved with him isn't even an issue." Getting involved with one of his teammates, yes, but him, no. "The league is really desperate for host families this year. And it just seems like such a nice thing to do, give someone a home for the summer."

"It's not like they're orphans," Tiffany said.

She mentions orphans at every opportunity. Part of the Miss Teen Ragland competition involves answering a question about how you'd change the world or make a difference or improve yourself. For Tiffany, it doesn't matter what question she's asked, she always manages to explain how she'd help orphans. Maybe her generous heart and not her generous, uh, chest helped her win the past three competitions.

I couldn't help but think she'd gotten her chest plus mine. But that was okay, because I liked to think I'd gotten her brains plus mine.

I looked at my dad, the real decision maker in the family. Well, okay, Mom was the true decision maker, but I knew if I could convince him, he could persuade Mom. It was the reason they'd been happily married for twenty years. They had communicating and understanding each other down to an art. I'd never seen them argue about anything.

"For two months, Dad, it would be like you had a son. Someone to pitch baseballs to—"

"I pitch baseballs to you."

"Someone to hit fly balls to—"

"I hit fly balls to you."

"You'd have a *real* boy—"

"He's not Geppetto," Tiffany said, "waiting for the blue fairy to touch us with her magic wand."

Maybe not, but I knew Dad had always wanted a son. What father didn't? But that wasn't the issue. The issue was: I wanted a boyfriend this summer, and to have a boyfriend, I needed to meet boys, and the Lonestar League was guys, guys, guys.

Honesty time.

I released a big sigh. "All right, so maybe I'd like to have a brother for the summer."

Okay, not so honest.

"A boyfriend is more like it," Tiffany said.

I glared at her. "Any chance you could move off to college next week? Don't they have summer classes or something?"

"I have three more months of representing the city as Miss Teen Ragland. I don't shirk my responsibilities."

Whatever. Her responsibilities are the reason I always have to bum rides with Bird.

I turned back to Dad and decided to just

say it like it was. "As I already explained, I don't want him for a boyfriend. I really want to host a baseball player this summer. Baseball is my passion. It would be a dream come true for me to have someone who lives and breathes baseball to live in our house. Think of the perspective on the sport he could give us."

Dad glanced across the table to Mom, his blue eyes peering at her over the upper rim of his glasses.

Mom was the one Tiffany and I had inherited our reddish-brown hair from. I'd also inherited her green eyes—intensified. Mine were a brighter hue. Tiffany's eyes were the same blue as Dad's. It was the *only* thing she and he had in common.

Mom shrugged. "I suppose we could make it work with a young man living in the house. But there would have to be rules—"

"Whatever they are, we'll follow them."

"There can be no hanky-panky—"

"Puh-lease!" Who said *hanky-panky* these days? "He won't be the one—"

"The *one*?" Mom asked, her eyes narrowing.

Why don't I just blow it here and now?

"We're just giving him a room, Mom. I promise. I wouldn't be interested in him if he turned out to be Johnny Depp." I gave an exaggerated eye roll. "Well, okay, if he was Johnny Depp, I'd be interested. But seriously, what are the odds?"

Mom's mouth quirked at that, because she had a thing for Johnny Depp, too.

"All right, then," she said, "you can have your ballplayer for the summer."

Yes! Deep inside I was doing a happy dance, but on the outside I did nothing more than smile. If my parents figured out the real plan was to get a boyfriend, they absolutely wouldn't go for it. Not that they had anything against boys, but Dad's always saying we shouldn't date until we're thirty. I'm not sure he's joking.

Now he nodded thoughtfully. "I'll talk to Ed Morton. He's the team manager, and I'm sure he can explain everything we need to do and get us the paperwork."

"Bird wants to host a baseball player, too," I told him.

She'd called earlier with the news her parents had given their permission for her to have a summer buddy, as she'd taken to calling him.

"Little do they know our ulterior motives," she'd said, like some evil scientist, which had made me laugh.

"I'll let Ed know," Dad said now. "I'm sure he'll be happy to give us a little extra consideration, since I helped design and build the field."

He winked at me, and I knew it was a done deal.

Chapter 3

*H*is name was Jason Davis, and he took my breath away. Literally.

Following the advice on the proper application of mascara, which Tiffany had posted on her blog at the Miss Teen Ragland website, I'd just finished applying my third layer—"one for length, one for width, one for beauty"—when the doorbell rang. Since we were expecting Jason to arrive at any moment, I knew it had to be him.

I quickly looked at myself in the mirror. I'd decided my boyfriend plans required more than my usual T-shirts, so I'd done a little shopping. New Gap jeans and a red spaghetti-strap tank with tiny white polka dots and a wide swath of white lace along the dipping neckline and down the center. My shoes were a corked wedge with a T-and-ankle strap. Really classy, I thought.

I'd taken a hot iron to my hair, but had only managed to straighten my straight hair further. But I didn't really have time for a do-over. Besides, my hair was a lost cause.

So, with a deep breath, I headed down the hallway and descended the stairs, trying not to clunk, but trying to get to Jason before Tiffany had a chance to impress him.

According to Stephanie, who was majoring in psychology, for guys it was all about physical attraction before anything else. "Think bright plumage," Bird's sister had said. "For guys it's all about sex; for girls it's all about love. Venus. Mars. Who wants to have sex with a dog?"

"Another dog?" Bird had asked sarcastically, which had ended Stephanie's lesson on what was important to guys.

Which was okay with me, because I wasn't ready to jump ahead to the sex part. Long, slow kisses were more along the lines of what I was looking for this summer. Really long and really slow.

So, it was important that I impress Jason

before Tiffany did, so I'd have an in with the team. In theory, I guess he could take both of us when he hung out with the guys. But if he only chose one of us, I wanted it to be me.

I could see he wasn't in the foyer and, knowing Mom, she'd probably taken him to the kitchen for warm cookies and milk.

The stairs ended at the foyer, the wall beside the stairs forming one side of the hallway that led to the back of the house. I couldn't see into the hallway from the stairs, but I'd perfected a swing-around. I grabbed the end of the banister for momentum and swung into the hallway—

Bam!

I slammed right into a big, muscular Jason! He staggered forward toward Tiffany—to whom he'd obviously been talking—and I crashed to the floor.

Technically, maybe he didn't knock the breath out of me. Maybe I knocked it out of myself. But who wanted to admit she'd been clumsy and too stupid to not look before she swung around the corner?

"Dani!" Tiffany said in a tone that clearly

implied, "Are you an idiot or what?"

Which was usually the line I applied to her following almost any comment she made, so it sorta stung to have her use that tone with me. I was way smarter than she was.

"You okay?" Jason asked.

And time stopped. Just like that. It froze, like a drop of suspended dew, just hanging from the end of a rose petal, and it was like I had an out-of-body experience.

He knelt beside me, his brow furrowed over the bluest eyes I'd ever seen. A deep royal blue. He was near enough that I could see a black ring around the outer edge of the blue and that little circle just seemed to make the blue all that much richer.

His face was perfect. Strong jaw, a little indentation in his chin that somehow managed to give his face personality. He looked tough, and yet he *didn't* look tough.

His dark hair was a buzz cut, probably because he played baseball during the hottest months of a Texas summer. His sideburns ran the length of his ears and served as a dark frame for his face.

Please, please, please, Tiffany, don't talk him into going for the Bruce Willis look.

He even smelled good. Like leather. I wondered if I'd be able to smell him in the guest room after he left.

And I was so not supposed to be thinking these kinds of thoughts! I'd promised Mom I'd have no interest whatsoever in Jason, but I could see now that I'd made a vow that was easier said than done. Who would have thought he'd be *this* hot?

As though someone had snapped their fingers, time started again.

"You okay, honey?" Mom asked.

"Gawd, Dani, get *up*," Tiffany said.

"That was some hit you gave Jason," Dad said. "Maybe we need you to try out for the football team. Lord knows we need a good tackler if we're going to State this year."

I wanted to die, absolutely die. Dad was talking about putting me in shoulder pads and a helmet. Rough-and-tough wasn't exactly the image I wanted to project. *Please think he's joking, Jason. Please, please, please think he's joking.*

But truthfully, I could see Dad seriously

calling the high school football coach before the evening was over. "Hey, Johnson, have I found some talent for you."

"I'm not going to try out for the football team," I grumbled as I struggled to sit up. "Sorry about knocking into you."

Jason grinned—a wonderful, sexy grin that made one side of his mouth hitch up a little higher than the other. "I have three brothers. Getting shoved makes me feel right at home."

He took my hand, and I felt a delicious spark of electricity cascade through me. He pulled me to my feet. I couldn't help but be disappointed by how quickly he released his hold. I wondered if he'd felt the same sensation, and if so, if it made him as aware of me as it had made me of him.

"So, Jason, how was your trip?" Mom asked, as though sensing something brewing that shouldn't be.

"It was fine," he said. "Thanks to MapQuest, I didn't get lost once."

"That's wonderful," she said, like it was a major accomplishment and she was really proud of him, and I realized that maybe we all felt a little awkward with a stranger settling into the house.

"We want you to make yourself right at home while you're with us," Mom said.

"I appreciate it," he said.

Could the conversation get any more banal? I wondered if he felt like he was in a bad episode of *Meet Your New Mommy*.

"I have a pitcher's mound in the backyard," Dad said. "Maybe you'd like to try it out after supper."

"That'd be great," Jason said.

"Maybe we could get in a few pitches before dinner," Dad offered, with much more enthusiasm. The blue fairy had indeed arrived and made his wishes come true.

"Actually, hon, later would be better," Mom said very diplomatically. "I was getting ready to set an early dinner on the table. I hope you like pot roast."

"Yes, ma'am, I do," Jason said.

"I rarely cook, but I thought tonight was a special occasion, deserving of extra effort. Tiffany, why don't you help me in the kitchen while Dani shows Jason his room?"

I couldn't believe it! Mom was actually handing me a few minutes alone with Jason.

"I'll be happy to show you your room," I said, sounding like the bellhop at a fancy hotel, noticing for the first time the large duffle bag on the floor at his feet.

He reached down and picked it up. "Lead the way."

"So, you're a pitcher," I said inanely as we started up the stairs.

The team manager had sent Dad an information sheet with everything he needed to know about Jason—emergency numbers, health information, but nothing that was really important. I mean, it didn't provide vital stats like eye color, hair color, or girlfriend status.

"Yeah. Didn't play that much this year because I'm a freshman. I'm hoping that spending time on a collegiate team, playing through the summer, will improve my arm."

I almost said something really corny, like I didn't think his arm needed improving, based on the way the sleeves of his burnt-orange T-shirt were hugging his biceps. But I refrained, since we'd just met and he might not know I was joking. Besides, it wouldn't have really been a joke because he was way buff.

"So, do you know the guys on the team?" I asked.

"I know a few, either because they're on my college team or our team played theirs."

"It must be hard to play on the same team as your rivals," I said as we reached the landing.

"I don't really think of it that way. Teams are redefined for the summer."

"Oh, yeah, I guess so." I unexpectedly felt stupid, and I didn't know why. He hadn't said anything to make me feel that way, but I just couldn't think of anything clever to say. I pointed toward French doors. "That's the game room, but we don't have any games in there. Just the TV. You can set the TiVo to record whatever you want."

"Thanks, but I don't think I'll have much time for TV."

Was that because he planned to hang out with the guys? I hoped so, since I wanted to tag along.

"Oh, okay. Whatever." Why was I so tongue-tied and nervous? Was it because the reality of having a guy moving in with us had finally hit me? He was going to be *living* upstairs, across the hall. "Your room is over here."

He followed me down the hallway, and I stopped in front of the guest room and did a Vanna White arm extension. "Our official guest room."

He looked inside. "Awesome!"

I'd known he'd like what I'd done to the room before he arrived.

My bedroom is sort of a living scrapbook. I could look at it and have so many memories come to life. The walls are decorated with pennants and pictures of baseball players and baseball caps for every team my dad and I have watched together. I'd selected a few of my favorite posters and pictures and put them in the guest room, hoping to make Jason feel more at home.

He walked inside and set his bag on the bed.

"I love that picture of Nolan Ryan," he

said, pointing to a framed photo on the wall. "The guy was raining blood, and he still didn't stop pitching."

It was one of Ryan's most famous photos — blood on his uniform after taking a ball to the mouth during a game. He'd had to change shirts several times as each one became soaked with blood.

"It's even autographed," Jason said, the awe evident in his voice.

"It's not personalized." Which was a silly thing to say, since he could obviously see it wasn't.

"Still," he said.

"Yeah, still." I could hear him saying, "Hey, guys, let me introduce you to my conversationally challenged host sister." But I tried again. "There's a shop at the mall that has all kinds of autographed memorabilia. Maybe you'd like to go there sometime."

"My budget is seriously limited."

"You can look without buying."

"Where's the fun in that?" He turned around and looked at me really intently.

At my eyes. He must like my eyes! He

looked away, then looked back at me. He couldn't keep his eyes off my face. His brow furrowed slightly, and it looked like he was biting back a smile.

"Guess we should go eat, huh?" he finally said.

"Oh, yeah." I sounded startled. So uncool.

"Is there someplace I can wash my hands?"

"Bathroom."

Jason hitched up that one intriguing corner of his mouth. "Where is it?"

"Oh, right! It connects the two bedrooms on this side of the hall, although the other room is the junk room, so you don't have to worry about anyone walking in on you. Tiff and I are across the hall and have our own bathroom." Although normally I used the guest bathroom, because Tiffany was always drying things in ours. "For your private bathroom, you can either go through that door there or come into the hallway and get to it that way."

I felt like I was rambling. I wanted to yell, "Someone shut me up!"

"Okay, I'll use the door in here, and meet you in the hallway when I'm done," Jason said.

"All right." I shrugged. "I'll wash my hands, too."

I really didn't know why I was so nervous. Maybe it was the way he kept looking at me, like he was trying to figure something out. Could he see through me? Did he know I wanted to impress him, use him to get close to his teammates?

I went into the bathroom across the hall, the one between Tiffany's bedroom and mine. Putting my hands on the edge of the sink, I leaned toward the mirror. "Could you be any more boring?"

Then I realized what he'd been staring at. It wasn't my eyes. It was a little ring of black dots where my mascara—while it was still wet—had touched above and below my eyes. I looked like some sort of Cirque du Soleil performer.

"Great! Just great!" I muttered.

You get only one chance to make a first impression. This wasn't exactly the impression I'd planned to make.

Chapter 4

During dinner, I did little more than eat and sneak sideways glances at Jason. I was kind of freaking out about the unfavorable impression I was certain I'd made on him. A klutz who ran into him. Not to mention the weird fashion statement. It hadn't helped matters that Tiffany had whispered, "Good, you got rid of the clown face," before we sat down to eat.

Meanwhile, Mom, Dad, and Tiffany peppered him with questions.

"Where did you grow up?"

"Round Rock."

"That's near Austin, isn't it?"

"Yes, ma'am."

"Now you go to the University of Texas?"

"Yes, sir."

"Great team."

Jason smiled. "Yes, sir."

"Do you have a girlfriend?" That, surprisingly, was from Tiffany.

I found myself way too interested in that answer. *For Bird's sake,* I told myself. I needed to know the answer in case she decided he was the guy she wanted to hook up with.

Jason blushed. "No. Don't really have time with school, practice, work—"

"Are you going to summer school?" Tiffany asked.

Jason's blush deepened. "Uh, no, but I'll be working."

He looked at Mom, then Dad. "The team manager arranged for me to work at Ruby Tuesday, so I can help out with the extra cost of meals."

"No, you can't," Mom said. "You're our guest. We have more than enough food."

"I'll be here for almost two and a half months. That's a lot of groceries."

Groceries? Not in our house. But I figured he'd learn.

"Don't worry about it," Mom insisted.

"She's right, son, don't worry about it," Dad said. "It's our pleasure to have a ballplayer in the house. You can thank Dani for that. It was her idea."

Jason looked at me then. "Thanks."

I felt the heat creeping up my face. "No problem."

We kinda stared at each other. He was the first to look away. It should have been me. I knew that, but I really liked looking at him.

"So, what are the chances of the 'Horns being NCAA National Champions next year?" Dad asked, and the awkward moment had shifted into players, coaches, strengths, weaknesses, strategies.

Have I mentioned that Dad's a UT alumnus? So, not only could Jason and Dad talk baseball, they could talk college, too.

After dinner, Dad's dream came true. He took Jason to the backyard so they could pitch the ball back and forth.

"You gonna join us, Dani?" Dad had asked.

"Maybe another time." Did I really want Jason to know I had a decent throwing arm?

So I went upstairs, grabbed my cell phone

out of my tote bag, and called Bird. "I blew it."

"How'd you do that?" she asked.

I gave her a quick rundown of all my most memorable moments, including the mascara fiasco.

"Like he noticed," Bird said when I was finished.

"Oh, he noticed. I've never had a guy look at me that hard before. He was probably trying to figure out if it was a birthmark, a tattoo, or if I was preparing for Halloween a few months early."

She laughed. Bird has a totally fun laugh that has a way of making you feel better, even if you don't want to feel better.

"I'm betting he was mesmerized by your eyes. No one has eyes as green as yours. Not even colored contacts can make eyes that green. Seriously, he probably didn't even notice the mascara," she repeated. "Stephanie says guys don't really pay attention to stuff like that. But I can ring her hotline if you want to be sure."

"No, that's okay."

"So, what's Jason like? And start with the vital stats."

"Black hair, blue, blue eyes. Tall, slender, nice, kinda quiet. Pitcher. No girlfriend."

"Fantastic! I can't wait to meet him."

I wasn't sure why, but I wasn't exactly thrilled by her enthusiasm for meeting Jason. She was my best friend. I wanted her to have a boyfriend. I just wasn't sure I wanted it to be him.

"What's your guy like?" I asked, anxious to move on.

"He's a hottie. Todd McPherson, but everyone calls him Mac. Dark hair, brown eyes. A little on the short side, but still cute. He's a catcher. No girlfriend, either."

"Are you crushing on him?" I asked.

"Not really. I mean, he's nice, and I like talking with him, but I'm not going to have a problem with him sleeping down the hall."

I told myself I wasn't going to have a problem, either, but I wasn't so sure.

"I've got an idea," Bird said. "Why don't you date my guy, and I'll date yours?"

It seemed like an easy and perfect solution. I didn't know why I didn't jump on it. Maybe because I couldn't see her with Jason. Maybe I didn't *want* to see her with him. "I don't know."

"You can't date Jason," she reminded me.

"I know." Mom hadn't made Tiffany and me sign a contract, but she had made us cross our hearts like we were five years old. Sometimes our parents just didn't see us growing up.

"They have their first practice tomorrow," Bird said. "I went out to the team's website and printed off a roster of the players. We'll scope them out tomorrow."

"Sounds like a plan."

A knock sounded on the closed door. Could it be Jason? What if it was? I hadn't changed for bed, but still . . .

"I've gotta go," I said.

" 'Kay. Later."

I closed my cell phone and set it on the nightstand.

"Dani?"

It was my mom. Before I could respond, she opened the door and peered in. "You okay?"

It seemed like an odd question.

"Why wouldn't I be?"

She came inside and sat on the edge of the bed. I pulled my legs up beneath me.

"You're usually the one your dad plays ball with. I wasn't sure how you'd feel about him playing with Jason."

I shrugged. "I'm fine with it. It was part of the reason I suggested we host a player, so Dad would have a guy to pitch to."

"You know your dad doesn't wish you'd been a boy."

"I know. But that doesn't mean he didn't wish he had a son."

"That's true, I suppose." She lifted some lint off the bedspread.

"Was there something else, Mom?"

She looked up, held my gaze. "You seemed pretty infatuated with Jason during dinner."

I felt the heat rush to my face. Did anything ever escape her notice? "I'm just not used to having a guy at the table, that's all."

"And the extra mascara before dinner?"

"A tip I picked up from Tiffany's blog. Obviously she neglected to mention it takes longer to dry with three applications."

She grinned. "You read Tiffany's blog?"

"She's the glamour expert."

"You're not usually into glamour."

"I'm almost seventeen. Don't you think it's time I was?"

"I think you need to be true to yourself."

I couldn't help it. I rolled my eyes. It was such a Mom thing to say.

She patted my knee. "I'll leave you with that thought."

Mom was really good about not belaboring a point. She got up.

"Mom?"

She turned and looked at me.

I scrunched up my face. "I've never had a boyfriend."

She smiled sadly. "I know, sweetie, but it'll happen."

I nodded. That was her standard answer, but I really needed more. "Thanks for letting Jason stay with us for the summer."

"Just let me know if there are any problems."

"I will."

After she left, I tried to look at my room through the eyes of a stranger. With the exception of my posters of Hugh Jackman, Green Day, and Chad Michael Murray, every-thing was baseball. I loved it.

But the important question was: *Do guys like tomboys?*

Chapter 5

"*I*s Brandon Bentley totally hot or what?" Bird asked, referring to the player standing at first base waiting for the coach to hit a grounder to him.

Bird and I were sitting on the bleachers at the baseball field, watching as the Ragland Rattlers practiced. A couple of other girls— "Summer Sisters" they'd announced as they'd walked by wiggling their fingers—were sitting at the far end of the bleachers.

"It is pretty warm out here," I said, flicking my fingers over the sash hem of my brown shorts. I was wearing a lime green visor that didn't clash with my lacy white camisole, hoping the neon shade would make me more visible in the stands.

Groaning, Bird looked over at me. "I think you should leave the smart comebacks to me. That one was too lame for words."

I shrugged, my gaze drifting to Jason, who was pitching in an area away from the diamond, along with a couple of other guys. A man I assumed was the pitching coach would say something from time to time, and one of the guys would nod. I guess he was giving them pointers.

Like all the other players out there, Jason was wearing a T-shirt and generic baseball pants. His shirt was white with red sleeves that stopped just above his elbow. No witty slogans, no rock band advertising, nothing to give any hint to his personality.

He'd come to the practice field straight from work. Apparently he worked the lunch shift, so he could make the late afternoon and early evening practices and games. It was Saturday, and the first game of the season would be Tuesday. It didn't seem like much time to practice, but then these guys were really only extending their baseball season. They'd already had months of practice and games. They'd be ready by Tuesday. No sweat.

Bird tapped the roster she'd given me when she'd picked me up earlier to bring me to the field. She'd added a column: Hottie Score.

"You know, I bet Brandon is a home-run hitter." She bumped her shoulder against mine and wiggled her eyebrows. "Maybe I'll let him hit a home run with me."

I laughed. Have I mentioned that Bird has a one-track mind very similar to mine? Guys, guys, guys.

"I think he's definitely deserving of a ten," she said.

While Bird wrote his score on both our rosters, I reached into my tote bag, brought out my chocolate chip cookie dough lip balm, and spread some over my lips. The summer heat was murder.

"So, who appeals to you?" Bird asked.

Dropping the balm back into my tote, I glanced over at her. "You say that like you've already made your decision that Brandon is the one."

"I'm narrowing down the field, that's all. What about you?"

We'd given Mac a nine point five, but only because Bird said we couldn't give every guy a ten.

I hadn't scored Jason yet. He deserved a ten. No question. But officially scoring him as the hottest of the hot would make me uncomfortable living with him. After all, I wasn't really supposed to be noticing him. A six. I could easily live with a six. Still, I felt like I was betraying him when I wrote the score on my roster.

"Shortstop is cute," I said. I glanced at the lineup. Chase Parker.

"I can't tell at this distance," Bird said. "I wish they had these guys' pictures on the roster."

"They'll have them in the programs on Tuesday."

The team always sold programs for a buck at the games. Inside were the stats on each Rattler. There was also a roster of the visiting team, but they didn't include their stats. I guess the general consensus was: Who cares? They're not *our* guys. Ragland was pretty loyal to its team.

"Opening night is free rattle night," Bird said. "Not that we need any more rattles."

Most home games had a giveaway. Opening night was always rattles that looked like rattlesnakes' tails on a stick. Big surprise — when shaken, the individual slats of wood clapped together to make a sound like an angry rattlesnake. Making them clack showed team loyalty. Paper fans were also a very popular giveaway, at least one game a week. Bird and I had quite a collection: seat cushions, team caps, team T-shirts, baseball bat–shaped pens, baseball stress balls — whatever the local merchants were willing to donate.

"I like the way the second baseman moves when he goes after a grounder," I said.

"Yeah, he's really fluid. I wish I'd brought my dad's binoculars."

"We'll be able to see them better once they start batting practice." Since we were on the second row, just to the right of home plate, we'd have a great view.

"How do you like having a guy in the house?" Bird asked.

"Hard to say. Jason is really quiet. For

some reason, I thought guys were noisy."

"I'm sure real brothers are. These guys are probably just trying to be polite."

"I guess. He played pitch with Dad last night."

"Must have been a rush for your dad."

I smiled. "Yeah, it was." Although Dad, loyal as ever, had stopped by my bedroom before going to bed to let me know I was still his favorite ball-tosser. "The guy's good"—he'd winked at me—"but no one can replace you."

His words had made me wish I'd tossed the ball around with them, but I didn't want Jason to see me as just one of the guys. If one of his teammates asked about me, I didn't want his recommendation to be, "She has a great arm."

"Is Mac working?" I asked.

"No, he's still looking for something, although I get the impression working isn't high on his priority list. He's all about the base-ball."

"Kinda like us, huh?"

Bird grinned. "Yeah."

"Do you think guys prefer girls who aren't?"

She looked at me. "Why would they?"

"I don't know. I just . . ."

"Want a boyfriend?"

"Yeah, some sort of validation that it's okay I'm not a beauty queen."

"Tiffany doesn't have a boyfriend, either."

"No, but a lot of guys hang around her. She had a date to the prom."

She had been crowned prom queen, actually.

"She doesn't seem real to me," Bird said. "You, on the other hand, are very real." She pressed up against my shoulder, pointed toward the field. "You know, they call third base the 'hot corner.' I think our third baseman might be the reason."

She was right. We had more important things to discuss than my sister. We had guys to rank, score, and rate.

"I never realized what a busy schedule they have, with games, practice, and work," I said. "We need some real face time with these guys, but I don't know when we're going to get it."

We got it a lot sooner than we'd expected. When the coach had yelled that practice was over, Mac had removed his catcher's mask, walked to the backstop, grinned at Bird and me (at least I think the grin was for me, too), and said, "Some of us are going out for pizza. Why don't you come?"

So, Bird and I found ourselves sharing a table and pitchers of root beer with fifteen guys. How cool was that?

I could picture the field during practice and exactly where each guy had been positioned. So I knew the blond on my right was the short-stop and the dark-haired guy on my left played third base. Thanks to the roster I'd almost com-pletely memorized, I knew most of the guys' names, too. Shortstop was Chase, the third baseman was Alan.

In baseball, the catcher is also known as the field general, and it was like Mac was in charge here, too. As the guys had been pulling tables together, he'd yelled, "Bird's with me, Dani's with Jason!" and he'd pointed fingers at us— like a flight attendant directing passengers' attention to the emergency exit doors—so the guys would know who was who. Of course, he didn't mean like boyfriend–girlfriend. He was referring to our families hosting them.

I wasn't sure how he knew I was with Jason. Maybe Jason had said something on the field or maybe Bird had told him all about me last night. It really didn't matter. I was now official. My first time being included with the Ragland Rattlers.

Bird had managed to get close to Brandon and was down at the other end of the table sitting between him and Jason. She'd tried to arrange it so we were sitting together, but fifteen thirsty and hungry guys jostling for chairs didn't exactly lend itself to a calm seating arrangement. Chase and I both dropped into the same chair at the same time, and we both popped back up way too fast, like a kid's jack-in-the-box.

Across from us, Ethan, the center fielder, noticed and laughed so loudly I was afraid everyone would know about the awkward moment. He said something to Tyler, the second baseman, that made him grin. Chase yelled for everyone to move down, because we needed room at our end of the table, only there was no place for anyone to move.

Alan offered me his lap.

I must have turned beet red, because my face felt really hot. Suddenly Mac pounded his fist on the table. He was sitting at my end, only one seat away. The thundering noise was attracting everyone's attention, and Mac didn't look happy.

"Parker, give the babe your chair and find another one for yourself."

I thought maybe Chase would argue. But instead he did what he was told and gave me his chair. Although he didn't really give up his place. He found another chair somewhere and wedged it between my chair and another one.

Suddenly I found myself up close and personal with a lot of baseball players around me. I couldn't have been happier. My plan for spending the summer in proximity to ball players was working.

"Lucky Bentley and Davis, man," Tyler said. "They've got a house full of babes. My family is total guys, not even a wife around."

I'd never actually been called a babe before, and now I'd been called a babe twice. Part of me wondered if they really saw me as a babe, and part of me thought, what does it matter? Once called a babe, you can always refer to yourself as a babe.

"So what do you do for fun around here?" Mac asked.

He looked way older than the other guys and had a shadow of dark stubble over his face. I figured he was a junior at whatever university he attended. Bird would know the details. I'd have to ask her later.

"We have a movie theater, an amphitheater with free summer concerts—"

"I loooves free," Ethan said.

"Don't we all, man," Mac said. He looked at me, rubbing his fingers together. "Until we make the majors, we're poor."

"Aren't most college students?" I asked.

"Yep. So we have movies, free music, what else?"

"Library, free books," I offered.

All the guys laughed really loudly, like that was the funniest thing they'd ever heard. But it was a good-natured laugh, not like they were making fun of me. Like maybe they thought I was really clever to offer free books.

"My kid sister has this book called *Free Stuff*," Mac said. "She sends away for all this junk: stickers, posters, booklets. She just loves getting mail."

"You guys must miss your families in the summer."

"Miss 'em all the time."

I didn't ask why they didn't go home for summer because I knew the answer: They loooves baseball.

Mac was really cute, with a dimple that appeared in his cheek whenever he grinned, which he did a lot. I was going to have to up his score to a ten.

The waitress came over to get our order, and we all went with the buffet—much easier than trying to decide on what type of pizza everyone wanted. While Bird hadn't been able to arrange the seating at the table, she did manage to maneuver so we were in line together at the buffet.

"I was hoping we'd be sitting together," she said, as she reached for a slice of Hawaiian Heaven.

I never understood why anyone would

want pineapple on pizza. I was a meat-and-potatoes kind of gal. I reached for the Double Trouble pepperoni.

"I already know you, Bird. Isn't the whole point in our being here to get to know *them*?" I asked.

"True. Listen, Brandon needs a ride home, and he lives on the other side of town," Bird said. "Are you okay going home with Jason?"

"Sure."

Back at the table, the conversation pretty much came to a standstill as the guys turned their attention to food. No Hawaiian Heaven at our end. Not much with vegetables, either. I might not have a boyfriend, but I was familiar enough with guys to know they ate a lot. But these guys ate like the planet would run out of food by tomorrow, so they had to stock up now.

As I slowly ate my few slices, I let my gaze wander around the table. There were lots of eights, nines, nine point fives, and tens sitting around. Any of these guys would make the perfect summer boyfriend. All I had to do was convince them I'd make the perfect girlfriend.

Chapter 6

"So, Bird said you need a ride home," Jason said.

"Is that okay? Because I could probably find another ride," I said.

"No problem. Makes sense. We're going to the same place."

I knew guys who exhibited more enthusiasm while waiting in the dentist's office. Could I feel more like a burden?

While chairs were being shoved back and guys were leaving, I'd been talking to Mac about cheap things to do in town, since we'd run the gamut of free things.

"Thanks for the tips," Mac said, grinning.

"Sure."

With my tote bag slung over my shoulder, I

followed Jason out to his car, a black Honda Civic. He beeped his key chain to unlock the doors, and I climbed in. It was early evening, the shadows had begun lengthening, and the car wasn't too unbearably hot. He had cloth seats, which were great, since I was wearing shorts. Mom's Lexus has leather seats, and I've burned myself more than once before the "cooling seats" feature kicks in. That's right. Her seats were actually air-conditioned, a skin saver in north Texas.

"So, do you know the way?" I asked, as Jason pulled into traffic.

"Think so. This street will take me to Haddock. A right on Haddock will take me to Leigh. Your street, right?"

"You got it," I said.

He glanced my way really quickly, before turning his attention back to the road. "I was surprised to see you at practice."

"Are you kidding? I'm all about baseball."

"Really?"

"Oh, yeah. Bird and I haven't missed a Rattler practice or game since the town got the team."

"I've never known a girl who was that into baseball."

"Well, now you do."

Tell your friends. Step right up. Meet the most amazing girl you've ever known.

"Your dad's great," Jason said, in what seemed like an abrupt change of subject.

"Yeah, I like him," I said.

Jason laughed. A deep rumble that just sorta rolled through the car, rolled over me, made me smile.

Also made me brave. If I wanted him to talk about me to the guys, I needed to give him some ammunition. I needed to do something that would make me a worthy topic of conversation. A little more alone time was needed, and since I'd gone several hours without an ice-cream fix, I pointed toward my favorite ice-cream shop. "Want to stop at Ben and Jerry's? I'll treat."

Five minutes later, we were sitting in a booth, each of us with a double-scoop cone. Jason was eating Cherry Garcia, and I was eating my all time fave, Chocolate Chip Cookie Dough. The scoop shop was also my source for lip balm.

"Speaking of my dad," I said, "Cherry Garcia is his favorite, too."

Jason looked at me with those blue, blue eyes. He'd raised his sunglasses so they sat on top of his head. "I hope I didn't sound weird, saying what I did about him."

I shook my head. "I know he's great. I live with him."

He leaned forward a little bit, resting one forearm on the table, like he needed it for support. "It's just that last night . . . I felt like I was playing pitch with *my* dad. I've never done that before."

"You've never played pitch with your dad?" I asked, unable to keep the incredulity out of my voice. I'd played pitch with my dad since my hand was big enough to curl around a ball.

Jason really concentrated on his ice cream. "My dad was never around when I was growing up."

"Never?"

I couldn't imagine anything more awful. My dad was an incredibly important part of my life.

And why had I suddenly turned into a question repeater? I sounded like some sort of game-show host trying to make sure the contestant understood the question. As a reporter-wannabe, I needed to learn to initiate the questions.

Jason shook his head. "Nope, he took off when I was a kid, after brother number three was born. It's always just been us and Mom."

"Are all your brothers younger?"

"Yeah, two are twins, a year younger than me, then my third brother is a year younger than them."

"That had to be hard growing up."

He shrugged. "Never knew any different, really. Mom was there, Dad wasn't. She used to play pitch with me. I always thought that was cool."

"That *is* cool. That she made time for you like that."

"Yeah."

He concentrated on eating his ice cream, and I wondered if he was thinking about his mom. I couldn't imagine being away from my parents through the summer.

"Why number eleven?" I asked, to fill the silence. In baseball, jersey numbers weren't assigned according to positions. Players could select the number they wanted. "Is it special or random?"

He glanced up. "Nothing too significant, really. I was eleven when I started playing ball, so I asked to have number eleven, like I thought I was going to be eleven forever. And I've just kinda stuck with it over the years."

Weird. The number on my softball jersey was eight—for the same reason.

"How was work?" I asked to keep the conversation going. Even if it was a downhill direction, movement was movement.

"Okay. Busy. Way too many orders for fried pickles. Apparently people here like to eat out."

"Oh, yeah. As a matter of fact, I hope you didn't think last night's home-cooked meal was our normal routine."

He smiled. "Your mom warned me that she has all the local restaurants on speed dial."

I laughed. "Yeah. It's kinda funny. Every January, her New Year's resolution is to start cooking meals every night. We're going to eat healthier: fruits, vegetables, low carbs. By the end of the month, she's back to bringing home takeout."

Then I furrowed my brow, remembering last night's dinner conversation. "When did my mom tell you about her speed dial?"

"Last night, in the hallway, after she came out of your room."

"You were talking to my mom? I heard you laughing. I thought you were talking to Tiffany."

"I talked with her a little later. You're the only one in the family I haven't really talked to."

"Yet, here we are talking."

"Yep, we're doing that, all right. Since you like baseball, I guess you know what a closer is?"

"Of course."

"Tiffany doesn't."

"Tiffany is so not into sports." She thought a baseball diamond was a type of gemstone. Seriously. Don't even ask how that revelation came up.

"She's interesting, though," he said. "I don't think I've ever met a beauty pageant contestant before."

I rolled my eyes. Even here, at my favorite ice-cream shop, Tiffany was getting the attention. "I'm not sure I'd call Miss Teen Ragland a beauty pageant."

Jason had worked his way through his ice cream and took a bite of the sugar cone. "So what is it?"

Suddenly there wasn't enough cookie dough in my ice cream to keep me happy. What kind of contest was it? Let's see . . . she was judged on poise, talent, and her love of orphans . . . oh, yeah, and her beauty. I sighed. "I guess it's a beauty contest."

"Have you ever entered?"

I couldn't help myself. I laughed at that and held up my hair by the end of the ponytail. "Me, Miss Every-Day-Is-a-Bad-Hair-Day? I don't think so."

"It's more than hair. I don't think I've ever met anyone who cares as much about orphans as your sister does."

If he hadn't looked so serious, I would have

burst out laughing again. "Well, there you go," I said. "Orphans aren't my thing."

He popped the tip of his sugar cone into his mouth and chewed thoughtfully, the entire time studying me like he thought I was suddenly going to change into a bathing suit for the poise competition. When he was finally finished eating, he leaned across the table until I was able to see the blue of his eyes up close.

"What *is* your thing?" he asked.

Chapter 7

$\mathcal{S}$taring into his earnest eyes, I almost told him the truth.

But the way I felt about baseball . . . it wasn't something I could share with just anyone.

"Movies," I offered, trying to get my brain to shift into witty conversation mode. "Movies are my thing."

His brow furrowed. "What, like making them?"

"No, like watching them."

"So if a judge asked you—"

"Oh, no," I said, waving my hand to dismiss the direction of his question. "I didn't realize we were still talking about beauty contestant questions."

Geez, for a moment there, I'd thought he

had a real interest in me, and instead, we were playing some sort of what-if game. I was so glad I hadn't gone into my spiel about my passion for baseball.

"Saving the environment, I guess. If I were a contestant, I'd want to save the environment."

"But if you weren't in a beauty contest, you wouldn't want to save the environment?"

"No—yes—I don't know. The environment is important. I recycle." How had we gotten on this insane topic?

"What's your major?" I asked, desperate to change the subject.

"Biology. I want to go into sports medicine."

"Not pro ball?"

"I'd love to play in the majors, but realistically it's a long shot. I need something to fall back on. How about you?"

"I think the majors is a long shot for me, too."

He laughed, really laughed. He had a terrific smile.

And I felt like I'd scored a few points.

"No, not the plans for your baseball career. School. What are your plans for school?"

"I've got a year of high school to go, and then I want to major in journalism."

"Cool. You like to write?"

"Oh, yeah, keep a diary and everything."

He leaned back in his chair, grinned, and nodded toward me. I expected him to ask if he could read my diary sometime. Instead he said, "Your cone is dripping."

I glanced down. Somehow ice cream had eaten its way through the tip of my cone and dripped onto my shirt. Great, just absolutely great. With a groan, I told him I'd be back.

I tossed what remained of my ice-cream cone into the trash on my way to the restroom. Of course, there were no paper towels to clean up with . . . just hand dryers. I rubbed my wet fingers over the ice cream, creating a big wet spot right in the center of my chest. *Oh, yeah, beauty and poise contest, here I come.*

I hit the hand dryer and bent down slightly, so the air would hit my shirt. I wasn't too tall, wasn't too short—like the little bear, I was just right. Medium height. Nothing special, nothing to really make people take notice.

The dryer stopped, and I hit the button again.

By the time I was finished, Jason was no longer sitting in the shop. I found him outside, leaning against the hood of his car, arms crossed over his chest, sunglasses in place so I couldn't read his expression. My tote bag was resting at his feet. Reaching down, he picked it up. "You left your bag on the bench. It fell over. Some stuff spilled onto the floor, but I think I got it all."

"Thanks." I took it from him, noticing that the roster was sticking out. My stomach dropped to the ground. Had he seen the scores? *Not unless he unfolded it.*

"I can't believe how much stuff girls carry around," he said, totally relaxed, as though he wasn't offended, as though he had no idea that Bird and I had been scoring the guys.

Thank goodness.

"We'd better go," he said.

Yeah, we better, before something as innocent as stopping for ice cream turns into a disaster.

* * *

"Hey, Jason," Tiffany said as he and I walked through the door, like she'd been waiting for his arrival.

Jason actually blushed, which I thought was cute. I wasn't sure I'd ever known a guy who was so easily embarrassed by attention.

"I'm thinking of going to a movie," she said, before we could move past her. "Want to come?"

It was obvious she wasn't including me in that invitation—her gaze was riveted on Jason's face.

"Thanks, but I'm beat," Jason said. "Practice wore me out. Think I'm going to shower and crash."

"Maybe another time," she said.

"Yeah, sure, I'd like that."

He would? Was it just going to the movie he liked, or did he mean he'd like going with her?

Tiffany watched him head for the stairs like he was her favorite flavor of ice cream. Had she forgotten Mom's rule—no dating the houseguest?

Then she turned to me as though just

noticing I was there. "Ed Morton called."

"The team manager?" I asked.

"Yep, he wants you to call him back."

"About what?"

"I don't know. I'm not your secretary."

Without another word, she hurried up the stairs. I hoped Jason had locked the bathroom door. Knowing Tiffany, she was hoping for an "accidental" locker room preview.

Oops, sorry! Thought this was my bathroom. I'm always confusing the left side of the hallway with the right. Silly me.

I walked into the kitchen where Mom was putting the last of the take-out cartons into the trash. Looked like tonight had been Italian.

"Hey, hon, how was the pizza?"

It suddenly occurred to me Mom had the habit of asking questions that really had no interesting answers. I shrugged. "Great."

"Good."

"Where's Dad?"

She tipped her head toward the door that led to the backyard. "Where do you think?"

I went outside. Dad was sitting on a cush-iony chair on the redwood deck, sketch pad in hand, no doubt designing a backyard sports project for a new customer.

"Hey, baby," he said as I sat beside him.

"Dad, could you not call me baby?"

He finally looked up from his sketch pad. "Sorry. Guess my little girl's growing up."

I grimaced. "Or little girl?"

He gave me a look that said he knew exactly why I didn't want to be called childish endearments, when I figured he really didn't know at all. What college guy would be interested in a kid? Besides, I was going to be a senior. It was time my parents saw me as I was.

"Want to play a little catch?" he asked.

"No, thanks, Dad. Not tonight. I was just wondering if you knew why Mr. Morton called."

He shrugged, stuck out his lower lip. "Probably to schedule you for concession stand duty."

I leaned toward him. "Excuse me?"

"Yeah. Host families are supposed to work the field's concession stand. Since hosting was your idea, I told him to contact you when he needed volunteers."

I stared at him. "If I'm working the concession stand, how can I watch the games?"

"I don't think you have to work the entire night or every game. The duties are split among the families."

"But you have a son for the summer. Shouldn't *you* do the concession duties?"

Dad gave me an indulgent grin. "I help with the field maintenance. You need to do your share."

I opened my mouth to protest, and he held up a finger. "You wanted a ballplayer in the house."

"Yeah, but I didn't know I'd have to work to have him."

"You know what your mom always says."

I groaned. "I know. Nothing ever comes easy."

"That's right." He reached over and patted my hand. "Go call Ed."

"Did you give him Bird's name, too?"

Dad grinned one of those big Bruce Willis grins that crinkled his face. "You bet."

Chapter 8

Tuesday afternoon I was at my desk, working on my column, when I heard Jason come home from work. I heard him go into his room and shut the door. I thought about crossing the hall, just to say hey. That would be the polite thing to do.

Only if we were supposed to treat him like family, then I should really ignore him. After all, I never went out of my way to welcome Tiffany home.

I heard Jason open his door, heard his footsteps in the hallway, then on the stairs. I wondered if he was going to raid the kitchen, but that made no sense. He'd just gotten off from work, and I'd overheard him mention to Mom that she didn't need to worry about feeding him when he worked, because he got a free meal when he finished his shift.

Mom and Dad were both still at work. Tiffany was off cutting the ribbon at the grand opening of an appliance store, which meant it was just Jason and me. Tonight was the season opener, and for all I knew, he might be nervous about it. Maybe he'd want someone to talk to.

I closed my file and went in search of him. He wasn't in the living room or the family room. Not in the kitchen, either.

Then I heard a sound in the laundry room. The washing machine starting its churning cycle. I'd used it a couple of hours earlier. I'd even used the dryer. Unfortunately, I had a bad habit of not retrieving my clothes until I needed them, which meant they were still there.

I looked into the laundry room. Sure enough, Jason had put a laundry basket on top of the dryer, and he was holding a pair of my panties—a red, lacy low-cut pair—like he thought they had the potential to bite him.

He must have heard me in the doorway, because he looked at me, his cheeks turning the same shade as my underwear. "I need to get my uniform washed . . . and dried. I'm not sure who these clothes belong to or what I should do—"

I stepped into the room, and without actually claiming the underwear as mine, I snatched them from between his fingers and tossed them into the laundry basket. "Yeah, I'll take care of it."

"Thanks." He backed off like they were radioactive. He was wearing a ratty T-shirt and faded gym shorts, the kinds of clothes I usually wore when I was trying to get everything washed on the same day. Except even with ratty clothes on, he looked good. Comfortable. Snuggleable. Yeah, he definitely looked like a guy that a girl would want to snuggle against.

"We all do our own clothes around here," I said inanely, pulling the rest of my clothes out of the dryer and dumping them in the basket.

"That's cool. Same goes at my house. It's just that most of the underwear is boxers or briefs. Definitely very little . . . lace."

I looked over at him. "Because you've got three brothers. No sisters?"

"No sisters. I'm discovering it's way different living with girls in the house."

"It's different having another guy in the house, too. I'm not sure Dad even comes into the laundry room unless one of the machines isn't working. Otherwise, Mom does his laundry."

Could we have a more boring conversation? I was beginning to understand why Tiffany fixated on orphans as a topic. It ensured she didn't spend time talking laundry. That was worse than discussing the weather.

"Sorry about leaving the clothes in the dryer. I didn't realize you'd need to do laundry so soon." As a courtesy I started to clean the lint filter.

"I probably should have said something. I always wash my uniform before a game."

I stopped what I was doing and looked at him.

He shifted his stance, as though suddenly very uncomfortable with his confession.

"Ballplayers have pregame rituals. That's mine. Washing my uniform," he explained.

"What do you do when you have a double header?"

His cheeks turned red. "Wash it twice."

"Do you wash and dry it, then wash and dry it again, or do you wash it twice, dry it once?"

"Look, I'm not obsessive-compulsive like some guys. I just like to go to the game in a uniform that's as fresh as it can be."

Which wasn't really an answer to my question, but I let it slide. "Okay, sure. I understand." Although I didn't really.

He gave a brisk nod, and I knew even before he spoke that a change in topic was coming.

"It was really nice of your parents to make their house available. I know it's not easy having company all the time. I'm really trying not to get in the way."

I waved that off. "Hey, we wanted you here. No way would we consider you in the way."

"Still, I know it has to create some stress, a little fissure in the family routine."

"Family routine? Please. We have no routine, other than Mom and Dad working all day, Tiffany doing whatever, and me doing this and that."

Putting his hands behind him, he lifted himself up on the washing machine, while I put the lint filter back into place and tried to decide if I should go ahead and start folding my clothes. No, that would mean making each piece of underwear visible and available for inspection. That was a little too personal.

Really I had no reason to stay.

"So what is this and that?" he asked, giving me a reason. "I mean, what do you do all day?"

"If I told you, I'd have to kill you."

He laughed. "So, what, like it's all a big secret?"

"Not really. I just always wanted to use that line."

"So what do you do?"

"Well, I have my own personal summer reading program. I have to read three books a week. Right now I'm reading *Marley and Me*."

"I read it. It's good."

"It's going to make me cry, though, isn't it?"

"Probably."

He seemed amused by that prospect.

"So you just read all day?" he prodded.

"I work on my column for the newspaper."

Now he seemed impressed. "You write a column for the newspaper? You mean the school paper?"

"Well, I do write for the school paper. I'm actually going to be editor next year, but I also write a column for the local paper. Before you think it's a big deal, you should know the editor is always desperate for filler pieces."

"But you get a byline and everything?"

I couldn't stop myself from grinning. "Yeah, I get a byline and everything. Thursday morning edition. Weekdays are usually slow days, and I think that's when he's most desperate for news, so my little column fills up what would otherwise be white space."

"So what do you write?"

"It's called 'Runyon's Sideline Review,' and I write about things that happen in the stands during different kinds of sporting events, from the perspective of the fan rather than the player. Gives me a reason to go to a variety of events, and I have a press pass so I get in free." Like I needed a reason.

"You're kidding?"

"I'm serious. For my next piece, I'll probably

reveal the scandalous secrets of the concession stand, since Bird and I are working the first shift tonight."

He grinned, like I was clever or interesting . . . or maybe just amusing in a she's-fun-to-talk-to-but-I'd-never-date-her kind of way.

The washing machine went into spin cycle, making a really loud banging noise, and he hopped to the floor.

"It's unbalanced," I said, like maybe he'd never had to deal with an unbalanced washer before. I know some machines self-balance. Ours doesn't. It actually starts walking across the laundry room, like it's possessed or something.

I lifted the lid and waited for the spinning to stop. There was a big sign on the inside of the lid: DO NOT PLACE HAND IN MACHINE WHILE IT IS IN MOTION. As though I couldn't figure that out on my own.

Okay, apparently guys didn't wash clothes like girls. I sorted. Delicates from nondelicates, darks from lights. Jason had simply stuffed everything into the washing machine. Lights. Darks. Jeans. Socks. Underwear. You name it.

It was a hodgepodge of clothing.

"I can do that," he said, as though suddenly remembering he had personal items in there.

He was beside me and had his hand in the machine, before I had my hand out. I was sorta blocking his view—at least that's what I figured must have happened—because he grabbed my hand instead of his jeans. His hand was like twice the size of mine and really warm. I felt this tingle travel up my arm and down to my bare toes, making them curl against the tile. Because he'd come around me, my shoulder was sorta curved into his chest. I could smell his leathery scent, and thought I could even smell fried pickles from all the orders he must have carried that day.

I looked up, up into his blue, blue eyes. He was looking down at me, like maybe he was only just seeing me for the first time. His brow furrowed deeply, his lips parted slightly.

I wanted to say something clever, witty, and sexy.

Because this certainly seemed like a kissing moment. If this was a movie, it would have been. It would have been the moment of awakening, of discovery. He would have lowered his mouth those three inches and kissed me.

But this wasn't a movie. It was more of an awkward moment, and I was pretty sure he was trying to figure out how to get out of it without embarrassing himself further.

Bang!

The back door to the kitchen slammed shut.

"Dani!"

Tiffany.

"Hey, where are you?" she cried out.

I so didn't want to answer. I wanted to stay exactly where I was and see where this moment might lead.

"Oh, there you are," she said, coming into the laundry room. "What are you guys doing?"

"The washing machine is unbalanced," I said.

"And it takes two of you to balance it?"

"I was demonstrating the necessary technique," I said.

"You just shift the clothes around."

Because I felt like I didn't have a choice, I

pulled my hand out of the machine and stepped back. I watched Jason struggle to move his heavy, wet clothes into a more balanced arrangement. Then he closed the lid. The machine went into a nice humming spin cycle.

"Great job," I said, smiling at him like he'd accomplished a miracle.

"Thanks." He was blushing, not really looking at me anymore, but looking at Tiffany.

So much for our almost connected moment.

"You had some news to impart?" I asked Tiffany. "Because it sure sounded like it when you came crashing through the door."

"I don't crash, but yeah, I have news. They've asked me to sing the national anthem at the July Fourth Rattler's game. Can you believe it?"

"Makes sense. You being Miss Teen Ragland and all."

"I've decided I'm going to do my own version."

I stared at her. "Your own version of what?"

"The national anthem. I'm going to sing it in a way that makes it bigger and grander than it is."

"I hate when people do that," I said. "It makes it more about the person than the song. 'The Star-Spangled Banner' should be sung the way Francis Scott Key wrote it."

"You're just saying that because you're jealous they asked me instead of you to sing it."

"I can't carry a tune to save my life. Why would I want them to ask me?"

She looked at Jason. "Don't you think she sounds jealous?"

"Don't put him in the middle of this," I said.

"Whatever. I have an appointment with my voice teacher, so she can help me develop my own style. Tell Mom I won't be home for dinner."

She flounced—actually flounced—out of the room.

I shook my head. I was *not* jealous, and I really *didn't* like it when people thought they could improve the national anthem.

I looked over at Jason. I was totally embarrassed that he'd witnessed my sister and me arguing. "Sorry about that," I said. "I'm sort of a purist when it comes to certain things."

"I hear you. I was at a game once where the

guy sang the last note for two minutes. I kid you not. I was really uncomfortable standing there wishing he'd just finish. Because it is our country's song. And then I felt disrespectful, wanting it to end." He shrugged, like he still felt uncomfortable that he'd ever had those thoughts.

The washing machine shut off. Wow, we'd been talking through an entire wash cycle. How amazing was that?

I didn't need to see his individual pieces of laundry going into the dryer, so I picked up the laundry basket. "Guess I'd better get these folded."

"Thanks for the help with the spin cycle," he said.

"You're welcome."

I headed out of the room thinking, *Could we sound any more domesticated and boring?*

Chapter 9

"$\mathcal{I}$ so cannot believe we missed the opening pitch of the season," Bird said as she tore open another package of wieners and dropped them into the steaming water. "I've never missed the opening pitch—not since the field was first built, not since the collegiate league came to town."

I poured more popcorn kernels into the popcorn machine. "This is only our fourth year having a collegiate team. So you've seen what? Three opening pitches?"

"The exact number isn't the point. The *tradition's* the point."

"I don't know why you're complaining. Brandon will probably play the whole game." First basemen usually did. He and Bird had talked a couple of times following practices. She really liked him. "Jason is the starting pitcher. He may be off the mound by the time we get out there."

Although I wasn't supposed to like Jason in the boyfriend kind of way, I was interested in seeing him pitch. And I couldn't stop thinking about that moment in the laundry room when his lips had been so close to mine. What would it be like to kiss him?

"Maybe we should have volunteered for the last shift," Bird said, bringing me back from the heat of the almost-kiss to the heat inside the concession stand.

"You wanted to see the fireworks after the game." Last shift did clean-up.

"I love fireworks."

The fireworks were another tradition. They had them at the opening game, the Fourth of July game, and the final game of the season.

"I know. I do, too." But I'd hated choosing between watching Jason pitch or seeing the fireworks, between working a shift with Bird or working one without her. Although truthfully, I shouldn't have any decisions to make.

Jason was supposed to be a nonissue.

In the concession stand, we'd been pretty busy in the beginning, as people arriving at the field had wanted to grab eats before heading to the stands.

Ours wasn't a fancy field. A chain-link fence surrounded it. The concession stand was a simple wooden building that looked a lot like the fireworks stands we saw on the side of rural roads when my family took trips across Texas. We had a slight breeze blowing through the open windows and a small, noisy floor fan keeping us cool.

As Miss Teen Ragland, Tiffany was involved in a lot of local fund-raising efforts. Maybe I should talk to her about raising funds to improve the working conditions in the concession stand.

Two host moms were taking orders and handling the money. Not that anyone didn't trust us, but I think they saw Bird and me as the grunt workers. They called out what they needed, and she and I filled the orders: Cokes (in Texas, all soft drinks are called Cokes), water, popcorn, chips, nachos, and the most popular item, hot dogs. Thank goodness all we had to do to prepare the hot dogs was slap a wiener in a bun and wrap it in foil. A small table near the concession stand housed the mustard and relish, so people could fix their dogs the way they wanted them.

As a rule, I didn't think anything was tastier than a ballpark hot dog, but smelling them cooking for more than an hour was causing me to lose my appetite.

"At least we'll have the party afterward," Bird said.

Her parents had agreed to let her invite the team to her house for an opening game kickoff party—although we weren't really kicking off the opening game, since the party followed it, but we all knew what it meant. An excuse to party. Of course, she'd invited the host families as well. She hoped most of the parents would be too tired to come.

Suddenly the crowd released an excited roar and thunderous applause.

"What is it?"

"What happened?"

Bird and I asked at the same time. And of

course, no one could see the field, so no one knew, but we kept asking until one of the newer customers, straight from the stands, was able to tell us that Bentley had hit a home run.

Bird didn't know whether to be thrilled for his success or disappointed she'd missed seeing it.

"He'll hit another one before the summer is over," I said, trying to console her.

"I know." She lifted her shoulders, then dropped them back down. "I really like him, Dani. Even though we've only talked a couple of times, we have so much in common."

"Three hot dogs!" one of the moms yelled back to us.

"Two popcorns!"

Using a pair of tongs, Bird grabbed one of the bobbing wieners while I snatched a sack for the popcorn. With an amazing flick and swoop of my wrist, I had it opened and ready so I could scoop popcorn into it.

"What do you have in common?" I asked as I squirted butter over sack one, then sack two of popcorn.

"Baseball, the kind of movies we like to

watch, television shows, music. You name it. Speaking of music, we've been talking about maybe catching a free concert at the amphitheater next week. He hasn't actually asked, but I've been dropping some blatant hints that I was interested. Stephanie says guys are shy about asking unless they know they won't get turned down. So I pretty much have done everything except tattoo it across my forehead. Anyway, if he does ask, do you want to come with us?"

I turned and placed the sacks on the counter, right beside this huge jar of gigantic pickles. Seeing the lengthening line, I tried hard not to frown. Why weren't these people in the stands, where I wanted to be, watching the game? So not fair.

I heard someone order M&M's. I loved the fact that all the candy was within the reach of the moms, so they could hand it out.

Mom One looked back at me. "Where are the Cokes?"

"I didn't know we needed any."

"Four of 'em. Two Cokes, a Dr Pepper, a 7UP."

I went to the machine, scooped ice into the

cups, and pressed a cup against the lever. I set the full drinks on the counter.

"Straws?" the guy said.

Obviously he was new to the field. "No straws," I said. It was too easy for people to toss them on the ground. Then litter patrol had to work that much harder to clean up the area. As much as I didn't like working concessions, it was way better than working litter patrol.

Another call came for popcorn, so I went back to fill a sack, watching while Bird opened another bag of wieners.

"The concert?" she asked. "You want to come with us?"

I shook my head. "I don't want to be a third wheel."

"And if the fourth wheel is another player? I'm sure I could get Brandon to ask someone. Pick a player. Any player." She sounded like a magician doing a card trick.

"How pathetic is it that having a player in the house was my idea, and I have to be set up on a blind date?" I asked.

"It's not a blind date. The guys know who you are."

"Whatever."

It felt like a blind date setup to me.

Another round of shouting, yelling, and clapping from the crowd drifted toward us. Quite honestly, I couldn't wait for our shift to be over so we could get to where the real action was happening.

It was the bottom of the fourth inning when Bird and I were told to grab popcorn and Cokes—our reward for serving time in concession hell—and get out of the way so the next shift could get to work.

We didn't waste any time heading to the stands. No reserved seating at our little ballpark. Tickets were five dollars—except when they had special dollar nights—and people just sat wherever. Bird and I found some bench space on the third row, right behind the home team batter's warm-up area. As soon as we sat down, we automatically reached into our respective tote bags and pulled out our rattles. I glanced back over my shoulder and saw my dad sitting on the top row—his favorite spot, because it gave him "a bird's-eye view." I waved at him, before turning around to focus on the game.

Ethan was at bat and Mac was warming up, swinging his bat. He turned around to face the crowd, touched his fingers to his batting helmet, and grinned.

"I think he's grinning at us," Bird said, wiggling her fingers at him.

Was he? It seemed like he was, but there were so many people in the stands, it was really hard to tell. While this was a small, wooden-bat league and we were a small town, the citizens did support any endeavor the town pursued, so we usually had a good crowd at the games.

"How about Mac?" Bird asked.

"How about Mac what?" Here I was, doing my repeat-question thing again. I really needed to break that habit.

"How about going to the concert with him?"

"Read my lips. *No setup.*"

"I'll feel bad if I leave him at home with nothing to do. I'm supposed to serve as his ambassador, right? So you'll be doing me a favor if you go with us. It'll be a group of us. Just fun. No pressure. No setup."

"I'll think about it."

Maybe I'd ask Jason, too. Maybe we'd

make it a whole team thing. Give me a chance to explore options. There were still lots of guys I hadn't yet rated.

Ethan struck out, and Mac went to the plate. First pitch, he hit the ball out to left field. A hard drive that bounced off the Backyard Mania billboard. Several local businesses paid to advertise on the boards that fenced in the outfield. Of course, my dad's business had the biggest.

Tonight we were playing the McKinney Marshals. We watched their left fielder scramble for the ball while Mac made it safely to first base. The score was three to two, our favor, but we could use another run. Narrow leads made me nervous.

The pitcher walked Tyler, almost like it was intentional. Maybe it was. I knew they did that sometimes when a powerful hitter came up to bat, especially if they knew they might be able to get a double play off the next batter.

And the next batter was Jason.

He was a lefty. With the bat held in place beneath his left arm, he lifted the Velcro on his left batting glove, tightened it, lifted the Velcro on his right batting glove, tightened it, took the bat, and stepped into the batting box. From where I was sitting, I could see his face clearly, the concentration, his grip on the bat.

Like so many other spectators, Bird and I waved our rattles. Our show of support. Then everyone quieted while the pitcher wound up. . . .

Jason just stood there as the ball whizzed past.

A perfect strike.

Come on, come on, come on. Don't strike out.

Jason went through the whole tightening his batting gloves routine again. He stepped into the batter's box.

The pitcher wound up. . . .

Jason swung at the ball and missed.

I knew even the best hitters sometimes struck out. I mean, if hitting the ball was a sure thing, it wouldn't be a sport, but still—

"Strike three!" the umpire yelled after the next ball crossed the plate.

I groaned. Jason's jaw clenched like he really wanted to hit something—the ball would have been nice.

Brandon stepped up to the plate next. With the end of his bat, he touched each corner of the plate, stepped back, stepped forward, touched the center of the plate. Took his stance. The first ball went past.

A ball.

Brandon stepped back, stepped forward, touched each corner of the plate, stepped back, forward, touched the center of the plate. He went into his stance.

I was suddenly aware of Bird gripping my arm.

Crack!

The bat hit the ball and sent it out over left field, out of the ballpark. Another home run. Another home run!

Bird was on her feet, jumping up and down, yelling, hugging me, shaking her rattle. I was yelling and hugging her back. Nothing was more exciting than a home run, even if it wasn't my guy who hit it.

When had I started thinking of Jason as my guy? He wasn't supposed to be *my* guy. He was just the guy living in my house.

Still, I couldn't deny that I wished Jason

hadn't struck out. I was a little embarrassed for him, which was totally silly. Guys struck out all the time. It was part of the game.

Besides, baseball was more than smacking a little ball over a fence. The other team had only two runs, which meant Jason must have done some impressive pitching, which I was certain to get a look at firsthand at the top of the fifth.

The next guy at bat struck out, which ended the fourth inning. Bird and I did another round of frantically waving our rattles to make them clack, the wooden slats imitating the sound of an angry rattler.

"Go, Rattlers! Woo! Woo!" we yelled.

I was excited because I was about to see Jason in action.

Only he wasn't the one walking out to the mound. He wasn't the one winding up and pitching the ball to the catcher. I was totally bummed.

"Looks like Jason is finished for the night," Bird said.

I bit back a nasty comment, like that her powers of observation astounded me. I knew I had no reason to take my frustrations out on her, so I simply said, "Yeah."

"Hey, you'll see him pitch against the Coppell Copperheads tomorrow night."

"Right. I'm totally cool."

Even though I knew starting pitchers didn't usually pitch two games in a row.

And I couldn't deny I was disappointed tonight. Brandon and Mac were back on the field. That should be enough. But I really wanted to see Jason play.

Bird nudged me. "So go talk to him."

"I'm not going to talk to him."

"Why not?"

"I'm here to watch the game."

"Oh, come on, Dani. He's probably totally bummed because he struck out. Give him a pep talk. You're hosting him. You need to show him support. Be there for him. Who else does he know?"

"My dad—"

Crack!

I heard the crowd gasp. I looked up. Pain suddenly ricocheted between the front and back of my skull. From far off, I heard Bird screech, felt hands grabbing me, saw the red, white, and blue fireworks bursting around me, and had a split second to wonder why the game was already over. . . .

Right before the world faded to black.

Chapter 10

Needless to say, I missed the real fireworks.

I woke up to find some hottie leaning over me. "How many fingers am I holding up?"

I wondered if he was just here for the summer and needed a family to live with. Hadn't I seen a recent headline: FAMILIES NEEDED TO HOST HOTTIES?

"Two," I replied. I realized I was lying on the grass. Hottie was on one side, Dad on the other.

"What day is it?" Hottie asked.

"Tuesday."

"What's your name?"

"Is the game over?" I asked.

"For you it is. What's your name?"

"Did we win?"

"Honey, tell the guy your name," Dad said.

"Dani Runyon."

"Good girl," Dad said, patting my shoulder. *"Woof, woof."*

Dad laughed. "She does that whenever I say 'good girl.' She says it sounds like I'm praising a dog. So she's okay, right? She remembers our little inside joke."

I thought he had tears in his eyes. Why would he?

"Yeah, she seems to be," Hottie said, "but you probably should take her to the hospital for a thorough exam. She's okay to transport in a car. We can take her in the ambulance, but you'll get billed for it, when it really doesn't seem to be necessary."

So Dad took me to the hospital. I'd never been to an ER before. I couldn't figure out why they called it an emergency room, because no one moved like anything was an emergency.

And the hard plastic chairs were so uncomfortable. I lay my head against the pillow of my dad's arm.

"You gave me quite a scare there," Dad said, holding my hand. His hands were rough and calloused from all the building he did. I loved them. They were incredibly comforting.

"I didn't know getting hit with a ball could knock you out," I said.

"If it hits just right, sure. That's the reason the city always has an emergency response team at the game. You never know, and we don't need lawsuits."

The lights were bright and hurting my eyes, so I closed them. "I didn't see much of the game. What do you think of the team?"

"I think we've got some talent this year."

"How 'bout Jason? How'd he do pitching?"

"Did good. Tired out in the fourth. They got a couple of hits off him. It happens."

"Did you call Mom and tell her? Not about Jason. About me."

It seemed like my thoughts were zigzagging all over the place. I couldn't concentrate on one subject for long.

"Yes. She was going to come over here, but I told her not to worry. It's just routine."

"Is that why it's taking so long?"

"Probably."

We actually sat for almost an hour and a

half before they called us into the examination room. Apparently since I was lucid, I was considered nonpriority. It was after eleven when I was released with a list of things to watch out for. (Number one on the list being inability to wake me up; yeah, being dead might be a bit of a problem.)

I was hoping Bird had my tote bag, because I so didn't want to have to get a new driver's license picture taken with this huge knot just above my brow.

Once we were in the car, and Dad had called Mom to let her know we were on our way home, he'd let me borrow his cell. I called Bird. The party was still going—I could hear it in the background—but no way was Dad going to let me go.

"Did we win?" I asked as soon as Bird answered.

"You bet. Six to two. Where are you? Are you okay?"

"I'll live, but Dad won't let me come to the party."

"Bummer. I want to see you, make sure you're all right."

"I'm fine. Just have a headache."

"I didn't even see the ball until it hit you."

"I didn't see it, period."

"I've never seen anyone pass out before. It was scary, Dani."

"It's something I definitely don't want to do again."

"Just a second, babe," I heard her say, then, "Brandon said to tell you the guy who hit the ball felt really bad."

"Babe?" I repeated.

"Yeah, we're sorta progressing. He kissed me," she whispered. "I'll tell you all about it later."

"That didn't take long," I said.

Bird believed I took thinking too seriously, while she was more impulsive. When we went shopping, it took me forever to decide whether or not to make a purchase. She made her decisions in a split second. *I want, I buy.* She was amazing to watch.

"I thought the whole point of your plan was to get a boyfriend for the summer."

"Well, I'm glad it's working out for you, because it sure isn't working for me."

"The season just got started, and you sure got noticed tonight."

"That's not the way I wanted it to happen."

"Are you sure your dad won't drop you off at my house?"

"Just a sec." I held the phone to my shoulder. "Dad—"

"Sorry, kiddo. Your mom would have a fit."

How did he know what I was going to ask before I asked?

I sighed and put the phone back to my ear. "Sorry, Bird. Did you happen to grab my tote bag?"

"Yeah. I'll give it to Jason. He's getting ready to leave, anyway. I'll check with you later."

"Okay. Thanks."

I closed the phone.

"There'll be other parties," Dad said.

Yeah, maybe.

When we got home, Mom was waiting for us. In typical Mom fashion, she overreacted, rushed up to me, and looked at my forehead as though she'd never seen one before. Although in all honesty, she might never have seen a knot the size of a golf ball growing out of my head like some alien creature.

"Are you okay?" she asked.

"I'm fine. I'm totally up for going to Bird's party."

"I don't think so. Not this late. How could you not see a baseball coming at you?"

"It happened so fast."

"Are you hungry? I could fix something—"

She had to really be worried if she was offering to cook.

"Domino's is still delivering," she finished.

"I'm not hungry, Mom, just tired. My head's kinda hurting."

"Sleep late in the morning."

She said it like it was a gift, when in reality, I had nothing to do except sleep late.

She kissed me on the cheek, and Dad patted my shoulder as I passed by him. But once I got upstairs, I didn't feel like going to bed. I was totally bummed that my night had turned out like it had.

I went into the game room and sat on the love seat. It was actually two rocking recliners joined on one side, so two people could sit on it somewhat independently. Recline or rock. Each had a choice. Before reclining, I grabbed the remote, turned on the TV, and started flipping through channels.

Five hundred channels, and I couldn't find anything fictional of interest. Incredible. I settled on ESPN, low volume. Closed my eyes. Let my thoughts drift.

I imagined Jason on the mound, preparing for the windup. He had pregame and at-bat rituals. He'd have a ritual at the mound. I didn't think he was a spitter or a jockstrap shifter. His hat. In my mind, I watched as he adjusted his hat, leaned forward, studied the position and stance of the batter, sighted the catcher's glove —

I heard one of the French doors click open, figured it was Tiffany coming to check out my latest fashion statement, and became a little irritated that she was interrupting my dream, but when I opened my eyes, I discovered Jason standing there.

He'd obviously showered after the game, before going to the party. He was wearing jeans and a Ragland Rattlers souvenir T-shirt.

They often tossed them up into the stands for the fans. I guess they gave them to the players, too.

"How are you feeling?" he asked.

"Okay. Just a little headache. The party ended kinda soon, didn't it?"

"It's still going on. I'm not really a party animal."

"No?"

He shook his head. "No."

"I thought all college students partied."

He shrugged. He was holding my tote bag and a Ben & Jerry's paper bag. He set my bag on the coffee table. "Bird asked me to bring that to you. The ball that hit you is inside. All the guys signed it."

"Really?" I asked, pleased they'd cared enough to do it, even though it was only a small thing. I'd buy a holder for it and put it right next to my treasured Babe Ruth ball.

"Sure. No big deal."

"And what's in the paper bag?" I asked in anticipation. I kept a carton of ice cream in the freezer, but it was at its best when it was freshly scooped out, packed down.

Jason held it toward me, somewhat self-consciously. "I stopped by that ice-cream shop on the way home. Thought you might need a little . . . special medicine."

Sitting up straighter, I smiled. "Chocolate chip cookie dough?"

He grinned. "Yeah."

"Just what the doctor ordered," I said, taking the bag from him and removing a whole pint of ice cream and the plastic spoon.

He sat beside me, and his portion of the love seat rocked. "The other night you said movies were your thing, so I made a quick stop by Blockbuster, too, and got a couple. Don't know if you're interested. . . ."

"That was so sweet of you," I said, deeply touched.

"I got conked on the head once, had to stay awake for a few hours . . . it was pretty boring. An aching head makes it hard to concentrate on anything important."

"So what did you get?"

"*Fever Pitch —* "

"A chick flick?" I asked, astounded.

"It's got baseball. Then *The Princess Bride.*

It's one of my faves."

"I've never seen it."

"You're kidding?"

"Isn't it, like, old?"

"Yeah, but it's a classic."

I wrinkled my brow, which made my forehead hurt. "Isn't it a chick flick, too?"

"It's got pirates and sword fights."

"Let's watch it, then. I think I've had enough baseball for one night." Words I never thought I'd speak.

"I didn't even think to ask if you had a DVD player."

"Does a bear growl in the woods? It's on the shelf above the TiVo."

Eating my ice cream—oh, it tasted *good!*— I watched as he walked to the shelf and put the DVD into the player. He'd made it sound like the stops were on his way home. They weren't. Between Bird's house and mine was nothing except other houses. He'd made special trips to get the ice cream and movies.

"Where's the remote for the DVD player?" he asked.

I stuck the spoon in the carton, grabbed the

remote, and held it up. "Dad has a universal remote. This controls everything."

"Your dad is into gadgets."

"Oh, you bet."

He returned to the love seat, sat down, took the remote, directed it at the TV, but didn't push any buttons. Then he leaned forward, planted his elbows on his thighs, and studied the controls. I thought I might have to explain them.

"What did you think of the little bit of the game you saw?" he asked, his voice low.

"I didn't really see much of it. I was working in the concession stand until the bottom of the fourth."

"Not my best inning. I let them get some hits, score two runs—"

"You know, there's no *I* in team."

He chuckled low, looked over his shoulder at me. "Who are you? Leon?"

I knew he was referring to a commercial featuring a football player named Leon. I'd seen enough of the commercials watching football with Dad.

"I'm just saying, baseball is a team sport."

"Not as much as some." He shrugged. "I don't mean to be a downer. I just hate having a bad night."

"Trust me. Your night wasn't as bad as mine."

"I guess it wasn't." He winked at me. "But it's about to get a lot better."

He settled back, raised the footrest, and clicked the remote. Funny thing was, I'd felt like my night had gotten a lot better simply because he'd walked into the room.

Chapter 11

Late the next morning I woke up with a thundering in my head that had nothing to do with the hit I took the night before. It was raining. Storming, actually. The kind of downpour that, if it continued throughout the day, would have the local meteorologists interrupting regularly scheduled programming to warn about area flash flooding.

Also, if it continued, the Rattlers wouldn't play tonight.

In frustration, I pulled my pillow out from beneath my head and dropped it on my face, regretting it as soon as the pressure shot pain across my skull. How could I forget about my—*wound* didn't sound right—my traumatized forehead?

I got out of bed, walked to the dresser, and peered into the mirror. Ohmigod! I had a black eye! An honest-to-gosh black eye!

The door connecting my room to the bathroom opened, and Tiffany walked in. "You okay? I thought I heard you squeal, and Mom told me to keep an eye . . . omigod!"

She approached cautiously, like maybe she thought black eyes were contagious. "Mom told me you got hit by a ball last night, but I didn't think it would be that nasty looking. Does it hurt?"

"It's tender," I admitted.

"I have some makeup that will cover it right up. No one will know."

"Maybe I want people to know. Maybe I see it as a badge of honor."

"Please. It looks like the first stage of turning into a zombie."

It may seem strange, because of her whole attitude toward orphans, but Miss Teen Ragland was a big fan of horror movies. Last year for Christmas, I'd given her a zombie survival guide, which she'd thought was hilarious.

I don't think she would have enjoyed

watching *The Princess Bride* with Jason last night. Correction: She might not have enjoyed the movie, but she would have enjoyed being with him. Even though he'd seen the movie before, it still made him laugh, and he had such a great laugh. In spite of it making my head hurt worse, I'd found myself laughing with him. I couldn't remember the last time I'd enjoyed watching a movie so much. Not the actual movie, just the act of watching it with someone else.

I turned away from the mirror.

"That is really hideous," Tiffany said, stepping back.

"Thanks, Tiff. Your attitude will help me go out into the world with confidence."

I sat on my bed and put my pillow behind my back. Maybe I'd just spend the day listening to the rain. Or maybe I'd work on my column, but change the focus to the dangers of being hit by a foul ball. Speaking of the foul ball . . . it was on my nightstand. I picked it up and began studying the autographs.

"Do you want me to fix you some lunch or something? I could call Jason and have him bring you some takeout when he gets off from work."

I looked at my alarm clock. It was almost one. I couldn't believe I'd slept so late, but between staying up to watch the movies and the rain . . .

Then I realized what Tiffany had said. "Calling for takeout is not *fixing* someone something to eat."

"According to Mom it is."

Too true.

"So Jason's at work already?"

"Yep."

I started tossing the ball back and forth, between one hand and the other. Jason had to be exhausted, although he'd fallen asleep on the love seat during *Fever Pitch*. I don't think that actually counted as his sleeping with me, though.

I'd ended up watching him more than I'd watched the movie. I wasn't exactly sure why I'd found him so intriguing, or why I took such pleasure in just looking at him. It was much easier to do when he wasn't awake and looking at me, too. Giving him a hottie score of six continued to haunt me. Maybe I'd give him a special score: ten point five. Just for being so considerate last night.

I looked up. Tiffany was hovering.

I waved my hand at her. "Go on. I'm fine. I can order my own takeout."

"You know, the real problem is going to come in a few days when it begins yellowing. Then it'll seriously clash with your reddish hair."

Only Tiffany would worry about properly accessorizing a black eye.

"But it'll go great with my eyes," I said. "Because yellow and green go together."

"Mmm. Might work. Still, come see me if you want it to go away."

And what was she going to do? Wave a magic wand?

"That thing could seriously affect your boyfriend plans," Bird said later when she stopped by to check out my shiner.

"Cheer me up, why don't you?"

"Sorry. I'm just saying . . . it's not what I'd call attractive."

"Whatever. It's not permanent. So tell me about the *kiss*."

She was sitting on my bed, totally loose, legs folded beneath her, shoulders kinda rounded, her smile one of complete happiness.

"Well . . . it happened at the party. I think the whole team was there. Dad was grilling hot dogs." She stuck out her tongue. "I'll never eat another hot dog. Anyway, Brandon and I were in the pool, talking, moving around just a little, and it was getting dark, dark, darker . . . and I didn't realize we'd gotten to the deep end, and suddenly there was no floor beneath me and I went under.

"Brandon's taller, so he was fine. He grabbed me, and I just glided back to him, and when I came up for air, he kissed me. It was so good . . . then all the lights came on. The ones around the pool, the ones in the pool. Dad had flipped the switch."

"Did he see y'all?"

"I don't think so. We broke apart so fast I almost drowned again."

I laughed, imagining Bird spluttering when she really wanted to be kissing.

"Glad you find it humorous," she said.

"He's not living with you, so it's okay to date him, right?"

"Do you want your dad to see you kissing a guy? It's just too . . . weird."

"I can't believe you got a boyfriend so quickly."

"Well, I don't know that he's technically my boyfriend"—she made quote marks in the air—"we've talked, we've kissed . . ." She leaned forward and grinned broadly. "I like him a lot. A whole lot."

"That's great, Bird."

Her cell phone rang. She plucked it out of her tote bag, looked at the display, mouthed *it's him*, and answered.

"Hey . . . yeah."

I felt uncomfortable looking on while she talked, so I got up, walked to the window, and watched the rain fall. The game would be rained out. No way it wouldn't be.

I tried not to wonder what Bird was doing right that I obviously wasn't. I mean, she and Brandon had connected almost immediately. Where was the guy I was supposed to connect with?

"That sounds great," I heard Bird say. "I'll let Dani know."

I turned around as Bird hung up.

"They've officially announced that tonight's game's been rained out," she said.

"What's so great about that?"

"The team's going to Dave and Bubba's, and we're invited. Apparently, the manager, expecting the game to be canceled, called the team owners to let them know anyone wearing a Rattlers cap tonight gets food for half price. Plus they have the pool tables and video games, so it's cheap entertainment on a rainy night."

And a chance to maybe, finally, at last, connect with someone.

"Brandon's taking me. He said Jason would give you a lift."

"So now you're arranging my car service? I could take myself, you know."

"That hit on the head has made you grumpy."

Not the hit so much as the bruising afterward. It was tender.

"When was the last time Tiffany didn't need the car? It's ninety-nine percent hers," Bird continued. "Besides, it's much cooler to go with a player."

If he was a player who wasn't living with

you. I felt like a charity case.

After Bird left, I couldn't stop thinking about her comment regarding my black eye affecting my love life. Since it was pretty much nonexistent at this point, I thought some serious intervention might be needed.

Going to Tiffany for help wasn't something I was really comfortable doing. Our interests were so vastly different that, sadly, our lives seldom intersected. I knocked on the door to her room.

"Come in," she sang out.

She was sitting with her legs crossed beneath her in the middle of her bed, all sorts of magazines and catalogs spread out around her, a notebook in her lap, pen in hand, glasses perched on the end of her nose.

"What are you doing?" I asked.

"Working to determine what would be the perfect outfit to wear when I sing the national anthem."

She said "working" like she was doing manual labor.

"It's a baseball game," I said.

"I'll be wearing my Miss Teen Ragland crown. I have to project a certain image.

People just don't understand everything that's involved in looking your best."

She gave me a once-over that said I was definitely one of those people with a low looking-your-best IQ.

"I can't believe how much effort you put into it," I said.

"You have no clue. For each appearance I do, I have to consider the lighting, what's in style, what colors go best with my hair, my complexion, how much should I tan, what style accentuates my entire figure."

I stared at her. "I had no idea."

"Like I said, most people don't. So what do you want? I'm sure you didn't come in here to talk about my wardrobe."

I felt kinda bad I'd taken so little interest in her life as a beauty contestant, especially now that I might benefit from her experiences. I decided a little generosity on my part might be in order.

"The game's been rained out, and the team's going to Dave and Bubba's. Do you want to come?"

"I can't. Wednesday night I deliver cheer to

the hospital—as Miss Teen Ragland."

She made it sound like the "cheer" was prepackaged.

"Gee, do you ever do anything as Tiffany Runyon?"

She laughed. "Of course I do."

But she didn't offer examples.

I stepped farther into the room. "Listen, you'd mentioned earlier about having special makeup." I pointed to my eye. "You said you could make it go away."

"Oh, sure. Sit down at my vanity."

As I sat on the bench in front of the vanity table, I avoided looking in the mirror. I flinched every time I saw the reminder of last night's mishap. The vanity's top was covered in bottles, tubes, and containers in all shapes and sizes.

Tiffany approached. "Turn around."

I slid around on the bench. She slipped her finger beneath my chin, tipped my head back, and sighed as though she'd just been asked to single-handedly rebuild New Orleans.

An eternity later, after countless "close your eyes," "open your eyes," "look up," "look down," "tilt your head this way," "tilt your head that way," and applying one thing after another, she stepped back and studied me.

"I'm going to have to do something with your hair. It just doesn't belong with that face."

"How can it not belong with this face?" I asked. "It's attached to the scalp that goes to the face."

She rolled her eyes, put her hands on my shoulders, and turned me around.

"Oh . . . wow," I whispered as I caught sight of my reflection in the mirror. Not only had Tiffany removed almost any evidence of my accident—the lump was still slightly visible—but she'd removed any evidence of me.

"We'll bring your hair down in front to cover the bump. There's no way I can make that go away," she said.

"Gosh, I look almost . . . pretty."

"Well, duh?! We share the same genes, you know."

"What can you do with my hair?" I asked.

"I don't know. That's going to be a real challenge. It's not even professionally straightened."

"Is yours?"

She creased her brow. "Yeah. How could you not know that?"

"I just never really paid much attention."

"I'm going to warm up the heating irons."

"Irons, as in more than one?"

"You're hopeless. It's not like the hideous nightshirts you wear. One iron doesn't fit all."

Shaking her head, she walked in to the bathroom.

I looked back into the mirror. Finding something to wear with this face was going to be a real challenge, too.

In the end, Tiffany helped me with the clothes as well: jeans, a lacy camisole, and a sheer green shirt that she provided. Because it was unbuttoned and tied at the waist, it wasn't evident that it was actually a size too big for me.

Tiffany worked a miracle with my hair. She fluffed, volumized, moussed, gelled, and sprayed it into obedience.

Standing in front of the full-length mirror in my bedroom, I hardly recognized myself. "Thanks, Tiff. Really, I just wanted you to cover up the black eye."

"Once I got started, it was hard to stop.

Kinda like painting a room. Once you touch the brush to the wall, you have to keep going until you've covered every inch."

As Miss Teen Ragland, she'd been involved in Habitat for Humanity. I don't think she actually worked on the house—although they did have a film clip on the local news showing her wearing a tool belt and a hard hat—but she'd confessed to me later they'd been props to make the story more interesting. She'd actually just gone to the site to "deliver encouragement."

I reached for the baseball cap hanging from a rack near my bedroom door.

"What are you doing?" Tiffany asked.

Holding the cap, I faced her. "I have to wear the cap to get a discounted price on the barbecue."

She snatched the cap from between my fingers. "You're not ruining my creation with a baseball hat. Pay full price. Beauty isn't cheap."

I looked in the mirror again. I wasn't even sure I could get the cap on over the fluff. "Maybe we went a little overboard."

"Trust me. We didn't."

I wasn't so sure, though, when we walked

into the kitchen where Dad was giving Jason pointers on driving in the rain, as though Ragland offered challenges he might never have encountered before.

Their jaws dropped.

Mom had been taking the lid off the tub of tonight's dinner—fried chicken. Even she looked stunned.

I felt a need to explain. "My eye turned black. I asked Tiffany to cover up the bruising."

"Well, she did an outstanding job," Mom said.

"Took me three hours," Tiffany said. "I need to get ready to go to the hospital. Have fun at Dave and Bubba's."

She left, and I wondered if I should go back upstairs, step into the shower, and wash everything off. Display my bruised face with pride.

"Do I need to put on a suit for this place?" Jason asked. "'Cuz I thought anything named Bubba's would be casual."

He was wearing a black T-shirt tucked into jeans. And his baseball cap.

"No, you're fine. I'm fine," I said, because I was sorta starting to enjoy that everyone was looking at me. "We can leave whenever."

"Let's go then," Jason said.

"Here, take this," Dad said, handing him a bright red umbrella that four people could stand beneath. "I know it's not raining at this precise moment, but the weather channel promised more rain later in the night."

"Thanks," Jason said, although he looked embarrassed, like maybe he was the kinda guy who preferred collapsible umbrellas. And who could blame him?

Thank goodness it *had* stopped raining. I was wearing sandals, and my feet got a little wet as we made our way to the car, but I could live with it.

Once he started the car, I said, "I just want you to know I'm paying for my meal, because I know it'll be full price, and I didn't want you to think I was expecting you to pay for it, because this isn't a date. It's just the team and the host sisters, brothers, whatever, getting together to have some fun tonight since it's raining . . . or was raining . . . it's obviously not raining now. And you're just giving me a ride, not a meal."

Shut me up! Shut me up! Shut me up!

He shifted into reverse, then backed out of the driveway. "I'm buying your dinner."

"No, really —"

"Dani."

It was the first time I could recall him actually saying my name. I loved the way it just rumbled, his voice so deep, so perfect. I wanted him to say it again, over and over.

But he'd stopped in the middle of the street. I figured any minute Dad was going to come barreling out of the house to find out what was wrong. I looked over at Jason.

"I'm buying your dinner, as my thanks to you for convincing your family to host me. Just accept it, okay?"

I nodded. "Okay."

He drove, and I settled into my seat, wondering what other surprises the night might hold.

Chapter 12

$\mathcal{N}$o surprise. I was the only one at Dave and Bubba's not wearing a Ragland Rattlers cap. Talk about feeling disloyal. And uncomfortable.

My discomfort must have shown, because while we were waiting in line to get our food, Jason took off his cap, folded it, and stuck it in his back jeans' pocket.

"You don't have to do that on my account," I said.

He shrugged. "I was taught not to wear a hat indoors."

I wasn't sure I'd ever met anyone who did things with so little fanfare. I thought about telling him to put his hat back on, but the truth was, it made me feel less self-conscious not to be the only one.

Like most barbecue places, Dave and Bubba's had a very rustic feel to it. The wooden walls were decorated with old license plates and the jukebox in the corner offered only country songs. The tables were covered in red-and-white checkered tablecloths, and the chairs were almost as uncomfortable as the ones in the ER waiting room.

The place was noisy and packed. Once we got our food—chicken, pinto beans, potato salad, and coleslaw for me, and the same plus beef and sausage for Jason—we went looking for a place to sit. Fortunately, Bird had saved us seats at the table where she was sitting with Brandon.

"Whoa! Where'd your black eye go?" she asked as I set my tray down and sat beside her.

"Tiffany covered it up for me."

"I'll say. I hate to think how much she damaged the ozone with all the hairspray she must have used on your hair."

"Thanks, Bird. You look nice this evening, too," I said.

The waitress dropped off a basket of hot rolls. I grabbed one and started slathering butter on it.

"Sorry. It's just a shock to see you looking so . . ."

"Pretty."

"You've always been pretty."

"Oh, please. Can we move on to another subject?" I glanced over to see Jason eating and talking with Brandon.

"Yeah, I think we better. I've heard of head injuries changing people's personalities —"

"Bird, you don't live with a beauty queen, okay? I know when it comes to appearances, I'll always fall short. And if you want to know the truth, I'm a little self-conscious about the whole makeover."

"Sorry," she said.

"Subject change?"

"Right." She looked around as though searching for a subject.

I hated being so irritable, but I just didn't feel like me tonight.

"Sorry," I said.

"Not a problem." She smiled, either because I sounded like my old self or she'd thought of a subject. "Hopefully the rain will end tonight and the games will start up again tomorrow. Three away games in a row. You interested?"

"Of course. I can't believe you even asked."

"After last night's experience, I'd understand if you wanted to stay away for a while."

"No way. What are the odds of it happening again?"

She leaned near and whispered, "No game Sunday. Brandon officially asked me to go to the summer concert with him. Our first date."

"What's tonight?"

"Tonight's a team thing. Anyway, do you want me to . . . you know?"

Set me up. I shook my head. "No."

"Are you sure?"

"Bird, they haven't even been here a week yet. I'm okay with you having a date and me not."

"If you're sure."

"It's not a big deal." Not unless we made it one.

As soon as we finished eating, we went to the back room where Dave or Bubba had set up half a dozen pool tables. Along the walls were pinball and old video game machines. I'm talking original Pac-Man. It was like this was where old games were put out to pasture. As a result, beside each machine was a bowl of tokens, which you used to play. They made their money on the beer people bought while playing.

Not that we'd be doing any beer-buying tonight.

"Do you play pool?" Jason asked.

We were standing against the wall, waiting for something to open up, watching as Bird and Brandon played at a table that had become available right after we walked into the room.

"A little," I said.

"There's a table. Want to give it a shot?"

"Sure."

We walked over and took the cue sticks from Chase and Ethan.

Ethan did a double take as he handed me the cue stick. "Whoa. I didn't recognize you. How's the head?"

"Not bad. Just a little bruised."

He grinned. "Glad to hear it."

Chase smiled broadly at me as he walked by. Was this how Tiffany felt, with guys always noticing her? Was it the makeup and hair, or were they just all glad to see I'd survived the conking on the head?

Jason racked up the balls and let me break. The balls scattered, but none slipped into any pockets. He gave me one of his rare slow, sexy smiles before bending over to the task at hand. He pointed to the red ball and then the corner pocket. Then he proceeded to make it happen.

Actually, I didn't mind watching him, watching him move around the table, watching his concentration.

"I think you can beat him."

I glanced over my shoulder and smiled. Mac was standing there wearing a jersey. Not his team jersey. This one had Mickey Mouse written across it, obviously a souvenir from a vacation at Disney World. "Hi."

"How's the head?"

"You know, I'm thinking about making a sign that says, 'I feel fine' and hanging it around my neck."

"So it wasn't an original question?"

"No, but it was nice of you to ask."

"Hey, I'm a nice guy."

"Your turn."

I jerked around. Jason was standing there. His smile gone, his expression serious.

"You missed?"

"Yep."

"Okay, then." I went to the table. He hadn't missed much. Other than the white one, the table had one solid ball remaining. The others — mine — were striped. I leaned over the table.

"Want me to help you beat him?" Mac asked, his arms coming around me, his hands resting over mine. "Loosen up."

I wasn't sure how I was supposed to do that with him being so close, with me being able to feel the heat from his body. I swallowed hard, barely aware of anything other than his directing the cue stick. We hit the white ball that hit a yellow striped ball that sent an orange striped ball into the side pocket.

"See? Easy," he said in a low voice near my ear.

"Think I've got it," I said, not entirely comfortable with him being so close. I didn't know why. Maybe because I was acutely aware of Jason watching us.

Mac backed off, and I moved around to hit another ball. But I must not have lined everything up properly, because again nothing went into any pockets.

Jason moved into position and promptly pocketed the last solid ball, then all the striped ones.

"How about letting me have a turn at playing Dani?" Mac asked.

"Sure," Jason said. "No problem."

He handed Mac the stick, then walked toward me. When he got near, he pulled the cap from his back pocket and settled it on my head. "It'll keep the light out of your eyes. Improve your game."

Then he walked out of the room, probably to get something to drink. I lifted his hat up, settled it back into place. It did help with the light, but I wondered if there was more to it than that. If maybe he was staking a claim.

"You can break," Mac said, as though my wearing Jason's hat held no significance whatsoever.

He beat me almost as soundly as Jason had. When we were finished, he handed off the cue sticks to two guys waiting to play.

"Listen, some of the guys have been talking about this free concert on Sunday night. I was wondering if you want to go."

"You mean with you?"

He laughed. "You see anyone else standing here asking?"

I nodded. "Yeah, sure, I'd like that."

He flashed a big grin and tugged on the brim of my cap. "Great. I'll see you Sunday."

He strode to the far side of the room and started talking to some of the other players. I realized we hadn't discussed details, like time, place, dress, but then I figured it would work out. And I'd see him at the game tomorrow. I looked around for Bird, but I didn't see her anywhere.

I walked out of the room and spotted Jason sitting at a table, drinking from a brown bottle. Was he drinking beer?

But when I got closer, I saw it was root beer.

"Hey," I said, wondering why I was either short on words or babbling when I spoke to him. I touched his hat. "Didn't help. I still lost."

The game, anyway. I'd won a date.

"Mac's pretty good at pool," he said.

"You're no slouch, either."

"It didn't look like you were paying attention."

In the beginning, until Mac had shown up, I'd been riveted.

"When I was looking at the program last night, I noticed you and Mac play for the same university," I said, doing our usual change-the-subject thing. "You must know each other pretty well."

"Pretty well."

"He seems really nice."

"He's a pretty good guy."

Not exactly a resounding endorsement. But then guys probably didn't spend a lot of time complimenting other guys.

He's the best. He's the greatest. If I were a girl, I'd definitely go out with him.

"Have you seen Bird?" I asked.

"Yeah. She and Brandon left. Something about catching a movie."

"Oh." I looked around, wondering what to do now.

"Are you ready to go?" Jason asked.

I nodded. "Yeah, I'm really kinda wiped out. I guess I'm not completely recovered."

"Takes a while."

He finished off his root beer in one long gulp. I was mesmerized watching his throat work. He set the bottle on the table and got up. "Let's go."

We went outside and stood on the covered porch. It was raining again. Hard.

"Crap, I left the umbrella in the car," he said. "Let me go get—"

"Don't be silly. I won't melt."

"You sure?"

"Oh, yeah."

"Okay, then."

He grabbed my hand—his was so warm, so large—and we made a mad dash across the puddle-filled parking lot. He had his keys out and was beeping the locks before we got there. We both jumped inside, through opposite doors, at the same time.

Laughing, drenched, and cold.

"I'll get the heater going," he said, cranking up the car.

"It's June, in Texas."

"I know, but I'm cold."

I was, too. I was shivering. Still, it seemed odd to use the heater in summer.

Warm air blasted up through the floorboards. It felt so good. Wishing I had a towel, I used my fingers to wipe the raindrops off my face. My wet face that had been partially protected by the brim of his cap. Which would have worked if the rain fell straight down. This had been slashing across.

"Oh, no."

"What?" Jason said.

"Turn on the light."

He did. I lowered the sun visor, looked at my reflection in the mirror, groaned, and slapped the visor back into place. "Turn the light off."

"What's wrong?"

I didn't look at him, didn't want him to see. "The makeup ran."

Not as badly as I'd expected, but I had dark smudges beneath my eyes and my bruising was more visible.

"So what?"

I leaned my head back. "I look worse than I did the night you met me."

"I thought you looked fine."

I rolled my head to the side, so I could see him. Hoping the shadows made it so he couldn't see me. "What are you talking about? I looked like a Cirque du Soleil performer."

"What are *you* talking about?"

"The black dots around my eyes?"

He shook his head. "I'm lost."

"You were staring—"

"Oh, yeah." He gazed through the windshield. "Sorry about that. I've just never seen eyes as green as yours. I was trying to figure out if you wore contacts."

"You were looking at my eyes?"

"Yeah."

"Not the makeup?"

He turned his attention back to me. "I didn't realize you were wearing any. That night, anyway. Tonight it's pretty obvious."

"Oh." Didn't I feel silly? "I thought—" I shook my head. "Never mind." On second thought . . .

"You don't like all the makeup?"

"I just don't think you need it. I mean, you look pretty without it."

Oh, really? That was totally unexpected.

He started tapping the steering wheel like he was listening to a rock concert, or suddenly embarrassed, maybe wishing someone would shut *him* up. "Sorry I don't have a towel in the car."

Subject change. He *was* embarrassed. How cute was that?

"That's okay. We should probably get home, anyway, and we have plenty of towels there."

"Right."

He shifted into reverse and did that thing guys do where they twist their whole bodies and put their arm across the back of the seat. Only his car had bucket seats, and his fingers grazed my cheek and then jerked as though they'd been stung, before he grabbed the back of the headrest.

He was staring at me, really staring at me, and I wondered if he wanted his fingers to touch my cheek again, because I wanted them to. I wanted to feel that spark again, that little spark I felt every time he gave me the slightest accidental touch.

"Do you like Mac?" he asked.

"Oh, yeah," I said really quickly, too quickly.

He nodded, looked over his shoulder, and backed out of the parking spot.

As we drove home, a heavy silence filled the car. I began to wonder if maybe he hadn't really been asking if I liked Mac.

If maybe he'd been asking something completely different. Maybe he'd been asking if I liked *him*.

Chapter 13

The next morning I went into the kitchen for an early breakfast and discovered Jason at the table reading the Thursday morning *Ragland Tribune*. He glanced up and smiled. "Secrets of the concession stand revealed. Call Oprah."

I'd never before been self-conscious about someone reading what I'd written, but I was this morning. Maybe because I kept replaying those few minutes in the car and wondering if I had really missed what he was asking.

No, last night it was probably just my imagination gone wild, because everything seemed fine this morning, back to normal.

"Yeah, I considered writing about the dangers of foul balls, but it would have ended up including too much of my first-person account, and the column isn't supposed to be about me. It's supposed to be about what happens around me."

"It's actually entertaining."

"You say that like you're surprised."

He looked like a deer caught in the headlights of an oncoming eighteen-wheeler, and I realized I'd really put him on the spot. What could he say to that? *Based on our numerous conversations, I was under the impression communication wasn't your strong suit?*

"Never mind," I said, taking the steam kettle off the stove and filling it with water. I was a British-breakfast-tea-in-the-morning girl, and I made it using a real teapot and everything. "I'm not fishing for compliments."

Okay, I was a little.

"I just . . . I just didn't expect it to be so funny," Jason said.

"You wanted a serious column about hot dogs?" I put the kettle on the stove and turned on the flame. "You want some tea?"

"No, thanks."

He was eating a bowl of cereal, some sort of bran flakes, with sliced bananas on top.

"I have a hard time coming up with a subject for a term paper," he said. "How can you come up with a subject to write about every week?"

"Well, for one thing, it's way shorter than a term paper, so I don't need anything with any depth." I sat at the breakfast table. It was situated in a bay window. Bright yellow balloon valances decorated the top of the window, but other than that, it was natural sunlight streaming in. Mom liked cheery. "Then I try to give it a quirky angle." I shrugged. "No big deal."

I didn't know what possessed me to say, "I actually have all the columns I've written in a binder. You can borrow it if you're interested."

"My own summer reading program?"

"Something like that," I said, suddenly more self-conscious than ever.

I wasn't usually one to toot my own horn, which could also explain the no-boyfriend-status of my life. If bright plumage was the key, I was closer to being a brown wren. Except for last night, and I'd certainly gotten attention then.

"Yeah, I'd like to read it," he said. "I can't

remember the last time I read for fun."

"Was *Marley and Me* required reading for a class?"

He grinned. "No, but that was months ago." He looked thoughtful. "That was probably the last thing, actually."

The steam kettle went off. I poured the water into an authentic Victorian teapot and carried it to the table.

Jason got up as I sat down. I almost laughed, because in a way it was comical.

"I'm gonna go run," he said.

"You can use Dad's treadmill if you want, so you can at least stay inside where it's air-conditioned."

"Your dad has a treadmill?"

I got up. "Oh, yeah. And an elliptical trainer, and . . . well, you name it, and he probably has it. Remember when I told you Mom's New Year's resolution is to cook healthier? Dad's is always to get into shape. The first week in January, he renews his membership at the gym and he goes three nights a week. By the end of the month, he's decided he'd have more time to exercise if he bought some new equipment for the house, so he could eliminate the drive time to the gym. By the middle of February, he's using it to hang his clothes."

"Are you serious?" Jason asked.

"Just wait. You'll see."

I led him through the house to my parents' bedroom, to the sitting area, or what used to be the sitting area, before Dad decided to get into shape a few years ago. I snatched a couple of shirts and a tie off the machines. "Knock yourself out."

"You sure they won't mind me being in their . . . bedroom?"

"You're not technically in their bedroom. You're in the sitting area or the faux exercise place, since Dad never really exercises here. But anyway, they won't mind. Make yourself at home."

He shook his head. "I don't know. I just don't feel right."

"Want me to exercise with you?"

He looked at me like it was a trick question. I wasn't even certain why I'd suggested it. "I can do the elliptical trainer while you do the treadmill."

"I guess that would work. Then I wouldn't feel so much like I was intruding on their space."

"Okay, give me two minutes to get some sneakers on."

By the time I got back, he was already running, working up a sweat. He had really firm legs. I figured he did a lot of running.

It didn't take me long to get going on the elliptical trainer. It always reminded me of cross-country skiing because basically I was moving my feet back and forth, holding on to the handles like ski poles, watching the miles go by.

I'd gone about two miles, after forty-five minutes, when Jason finally went into cool-down mode.

"A lot better than running outside," he said, breathless.

"That was Dad's theory behind getting the equipment, but as you can see, he found other uses for it."

Jason laughed. "If your dad is really serious about getting into shape, I could help get him on a program. You know, ask him to work out with me."

"For any exercise program to work, doesn't the person have to be self-motivated? I mean, doesn't Dad need to take the first step?"

"Yeah, I guess so." He took a gulp from his water bottle, then wiped a hand towel over his face.

"So you think it's okay if I use the equipment every morning?" he asked.

"Oh, sure. Mom and Dad are usually out of the house by eight." And I'd add exercising to my morning routine, so he wouldn't feel uncomfortable being in their bedroom. It was the good hostess thing to do.

"What about the backyard stuff?" he asked.

"What about it?"

"Is it okay if I use it, too?"

"Oh, sure. The equipment is in a metal shed in the back. Just help yourself. It's not locked or anything. And if you want company, just let me know. I'll be happy to play with you."

Did I just say that? I did not just say that. Like we were six years old and heading for a sandbox.

He was grinning again, like he thought it was funny or stupid or I was having a Tiffany moment.

"I didn't mean play with you exactly," I said. "I meant . . . you know, keep you company so you don't feel awkward . . . you know, like I exercised with you."

"I'll be okay alone in the backyard." He stepped off the treadmill. "I'm going to go shower."

He waited a heartbeat, like he expected me to say I'd be happy to keep him company in the shower, too.

Fortunately, my brain finally kicked in, and I kept my mouth shut.

I watched him walk out of the room. I thought I'd known everything that would be involved in having a baseball player living with us for the summer.

I was discovering that I didn't have a clue.

Chapter 14

"I knew Mac was interested in you," Bird said late the next morning.

We were at Stonebridge Mall. Having decided the concert Sunday night would be our first official summer dates, we wanted new outfits to mark the occasion.

"But was he interested before Wednesday night?" I asked.

"What are you asking?"

"I was a Tiffany clone."

"I don't get what you're saying. He talked to you the night we went out for pizza."

"I know, but he didn't ask me out then. As a matter of fact, he was more interested in learning about free and cheap stuff than learning about me."

"He smiled at you during the first game. Remember? From the batter's box?"

"How do you know it was me? It could have been you. Or my dad, even. The stands were packed."

He'd done the same thing at last night's game, which they'd won, whenever he first got into the batter's box. I was beginning to wonder if maybe it was his good-luck ritual.

Bird stopped walking and faced me. "What do you want? He asked you out. You have a date. A real chance at a boyfriend."

I guess I wanted it to *feel* like it was a real chance. But it just didn't.

"You're thinking about it too much, Dani," Bird said. "He likes you. You like him."

An awful thought occurred to me. "You didn't tell him to ask me out, did you?"

"Of course not. Now will you stop worrying about it and start worrying about what you're going to wear Sunday? We don't have a lot of time if we're going to the game tonight."

Actually, we had quite a bit of time. The nice thing about the Lonestar League was that even the out-of-town games were nearby, within a short driving distance, sometimes no more than half an hour away.

"We're definitely going to the game tonight," I said.

"Jason will probably pitch," Bird said.

"I hope so." He hadn't last night. I really wanted to see him in action.

"Oh, look at these shoes," Bird said. "Aren't they to die for?"

They were fuchsia sequined sandals with a wide platform and four-inch heels.

"I've gotta have them," she said, zipping into the store.

"What will you wear them with?" I asked, following after her.

"I'll find something."

I loved that about Bird. When I went shopping with Tiffany, she never bought anything unless she knew exactly what she was going to wear with it. Bird bought things simply because she liked them.

"You have to find something," she said when the clerk went to get her shoes in a size five.

Unfortunately, the only thing that really

appealed to me was a pair of sneakers with light brown leather and mesh. For my date with Mac, I wanted something girly, and they absolutely weren't.

"How about these?" Bird asked, holding up a pair of clogs with a crocheted upper.

I loved them! But would Mac? Was he expecting more of a Tiffany look? Was that what he wanted? Was that what I should deliver?

I wrinkled my nose and turned to some open-toed spiked heels. "I think these might go with my denim capris."

"You're not serious, are you?" she asked. "We'll be walking on grass. Remember at your grandma's funeral, when you wore heels, and one shoe sank into the dirt, and you ended up going shoeless to the grave site?"

Truthfully, I didn't remember a whole lot about my grandma's funeral except how much it had hurt to lose her.

"Go with the clogs," she said, her voice no longer near me.

I looked back; she was modeling the sequined sandals.

"Think I can find nail polish to match the sequins?" she asked.

"Oh, yeah," I assured her. Bird could find anything.

"I'll take them," she said to the clerk, before turning to me. "What about you?"

Forty-five minutes later, after having tried on eight different pairs of shoes, I left with the crocheted clogs and the sneakers.

"You were trying on shoes that Tiffany would wear," Bird said when we were strolling back through the mall.

And every one of them had been incredibly uncomfortable. How did she do it?

"After last night, I'm just thinking maybe more feminine is the way to go."

"You're not going to start entering the Miss Teen Ragland contest, are you?"

"Of course not."

"Oh, look at this camisole! Can you believe it?" Bird asked.

It was fuchsia with a row of sequins along the front. Laughing, I let Bird pull me into the store. With any luck, maybe she'd find me something to match my clogs.

An hour later, we were in the parking lot, walking to Bird's car, when her cell phone rang.

"Hey!" she said, smiling so brightly that I didn't have to ask who was calling her.

"You're kidding! Bummer! Oh, I know, I know, I can't believe it. Dani's with me."

Having someone talk on her cell while you're standing next to her is a little like getting a manicure and having the lady doing your nails speak in a foreign language to the manicurist on the other side of you. You know she's saying something unflattering about your nails. Otherwise, why not talk in English?

I could just imagine what was being said . . .

Brandon: *"Mac's changed his mind about going out with Dani."*

Bird: *"You're kidding!"*

Brandon: *"Jason told him she was a loser."*

Bird: *"Bummer!"*

Brandon: *"We're only here for the summer. Time is short. We've gotta make the most of it."*

Bird: *"Oh, I know, I know."*

Brandon: *"Mac's going to be a no-show Sunday night."*

Bird: *"I can't believe it. Dani's with me."*

"Okay, meet you there," Bird said. She snapped her cell closed. "That was Brandon."

"I never would have guessed. So, what couldn't you believe?" I asked, my stomach clenching as I wondered if I'd accurately guessed his side of the conversation.

"It's his story to tell. Come on, we're going to have lunch with him."

I shook my head. "He doesn't want me there. Take me home first."

"I told him you were with me. He's cool with it. A couple of the other guys are with him, so it's not like we'd be staring into each other's eyes across the table."

She unlocked her door and scrambled inside. I hurried around to the passenger side and slid in.

"I mean, you have to eat, right?" she said.

"If you're sure I won't be a third wheel."

"Dani, you're my best friend. You'd never be a third wheel."

She started the car.

"So where are we going?"

"Ruby Tuesday. Jason's working lunch and he promised them a discount."

* * *

I couldn't believe it. The couple of other guys Bird had alluded to turned out to be only one other guy: Mac.

He and Brandon were in a booth, sitting opposite each other, which meant when Bird and I got there, seating was pre-determined. Bird sat by Brandon and I sat by Mac.

He really *was* hot. He kinda leaned back in the corner. I wasn't sure if it was to give me more room or so he could get a better angle to look at me. I decided to believe it was the latter. And I could only hope he wasn't wondering if I was the same girl he'd asked out. Today I was sans makeup—not having realized I'd be seeing him.

"I can't believe you quit your job after only half a day," Bird said to Brandon. She looked at me. "He and Mac got a call last night. A temp job was available—"

"—at Tommy's Fertilizing Plant," Brandon interrupted. "They said it was hauling stuff. I thought we'd be hauling bags of fertilizer out to trucks or something."

"It's *making* fertilizer," Mac said. "You

know what they use to make fertilizer?"

"Manure?" I offered.

"The plant wasn't air-conditioned. It's ninety-eight degrees in the shade," Brandon said. "I want some spending money, but no one could pay me enough to shovel that sh—"

"Hey, guys," Jason said, setting a plate of fried pickles on the table. "What do you girls want to drink?"

"Sweet tea," Bird and I said at the same time.

I was glad I had something to say, because I was feeling a little self-conscious sitting so close to Mac, especially when it seemed like Jason was trying really hard not to look at me. I wondered why.

"Know what you want to order?" he asked.

Everyone else ordered burgers. I almost went with a salad because that's what Tiffany would order, but in the end, I went with an artery clogger: double-cheese quesadillas.

When he walked off, I felt a little badly that he had to work, and we were there with nothing to do except have a good time.

"Tell me you showered before you came over," Bird said.

"Most definitely," Brandon said, picking up a pickle and dipping it into the Ranch dressing.

"You could come work for me," Bird said. Three years ago, Bird had started her own business: Scoopin' Poopin.' She'd gone to dog owners in her neighborhood and offered to clean out their backyards each week for a monthly fee. Once she'd turned sixteen and could drive, she'd expanded her business beyond the neighborhood.

"It's still shoveling—" Brandon began.

"It's not the same," Bird said. "I do it really early in the morning before it gets hot, and I have a long-handled scooper."

Brandon grinned. "Thanks, babe, but we'll find something."

I could tell he was humoring her. The thing was, Bird's business was actually doing quite well, and she'd already put aside a hefty chunk into her savings. She'd offered to make me a partner, but as usual I'd thought about it too long and missed the opportunity, which served me right for not having faith in her idea to begin with.

A waitress brought our teas over.

"I guess we could wait tables somewhere, too," Mac said.

"Don't sweat it. We'll find something," Brandon said. "Something where we don't have to sweat."

"Help yourself to a pickle," Mac said. "They're on the house, according to Jason."

"Won't he get into trouble giving us free food?" I asked.

"I'm sure he okay'd it with the manager," Brandon said. "Besides, we're the heroes of Ragland, right?"

"You're my hero," Bird said. It sounded so unBirdlike, to hear her gushing over a guy, saying a corny line like she was starring in a bad movie.

"Here you go, guys," Jason said, handing out our food.

He'd carried it over on a huge brown tray, setting it on a stand. I was majorly impressed with his ability to make it look like the weight was nothing.

"You guys need anything else?" he asked.

"Think we've got it all. When you get a

break, why don't you come join us?" Brandon asked.

"It's gonna be a while. We're pretty busy right now."

He still seemed to be avoiding looking at me.

"We're not in any hurry," Brandon said. "If you get a chance, come over."

Jason nodded before walking away to take care of people at another table.

"That dude is so shy, man," Mac said.

I looked at him, probably like he'd spoken a foreign language. "What?"

"He's really shy." He sprinkled salt and pepper on his burger, leaving all the vegetables off to the side, before putting the top bun in place.

Bird gave me a look that seemed to say, "Did you not realize that?"

No, I hadn't really realized it. I knew he blushed easily, and he was quiet, but we'd talked.

"Want one of my fries?" Mac asked.

I looked over at him. Since he was chewing,

he was smiling more with his eyes than his mouth. And Sunday night we had a date.

"Sure," I said, taking a fry and dipping it in his ketchup. "And you can have some of my quesadilla if you want."

Just like a real couple: sharing food. Before another week went by, I might actually find myself with a boyfriend.

Chapter 15

Saturday night, against the Plano Blue Sox, I finally, finally got to watch Jason pitch. I felt the same high I'd experienced the first time my dad took me to watch Roger Clemens play. Okay, maybe I was actually a little more excited about watching Jason pitch. I loved his windup and concentration. I loved the way, before each pitch, he lifted his cap off his head, settled it into place, then tugged on the brim, exactly as he'd tugged on it when he'd placed it on my head at Dave and Bubba's.

Bird and I were sitting in the bleachers. It was the top of the third, and Jason was still on the mound. He was having a terrific game. Three batters up, three down. A no-hitter so far. He should have looked happier. Instead, he looked majorly ticked off. I guessed maybe it was a guy thing. Stay serious, stay focused. Look mean.

"Strike three!" the ump yelled, and that was the end of another no-hit inning for Jason.

"Watch Brandon run across the field," Bird said.

He made a beeline for the pitcher's mound, did a little leap over it, and ran to the dugout.

"He does that every time," Bird said.

"Why?"

"Says it brings him luck. He is so superstitious. He won't wash his game socks as long as the team is winning."

"Ew! And he didn't want to work in a fertilizer plant?"

"I know. Go figure."

I watched Jason come in from the field. No one talked to him, no one high-fived him. He was having an absolutely wonderful game and he was being completely ignored, sitting in the corner of the dugout. Alone. Alternately lifting the Velcro on his batting gloves and pressing it back into place, which seemed odd when he'd batted last inning. Unless we encountered a hitting streak, he wouldn't be batting this inning. So why was he focusing so hard on his gloves and not watching the game?

We'd had a couple of hits, but no runs. So the game was tied zero–zero.

"Hey, listen," Bird said, cutting into my thoughts, "I was looking at the concession stand volunteer roster. You and I need to volunteer to work again soon, so we don't get scheduled to work during the July Fourth game. That game is just too much fun with dollar hot dogs—"

"Too much work, you mean, with the hot dogs on special."

"Can you imagine? Everything is a buck that night. People will go crazy buying, and we'll go crazy working. So let's do some early volunteering so we're off-duty that night. Besides, you've already missed one set of summer fireworks. No reason for you to risk missing another."

Crack!

I covered my head, ducked down. Bird didn't laugh. She likened me to a survivor of some traumatic event who is always spooked by certain noises.

She just touched my shoulder and said, "It went the other way."

I straightened up. "But it *was* a foul ball."

"Yeah."

I hated that I kept flinching. I wondered how long it was going to take before I could totally relax at a game.

Alan was at bat. The next time he swung, he connected and sent the ball in a line drive down the grass between center and left field. They both scrambled for it. By the time one of them got it, Alan was safe at first.

"Why do you think they're ignoring Jason?" I asked.

"I don't know. Go down there and talk to him," Bird suggested.

"I'm not going to do that."

"Why not?"

I shrugged. "We're here to watch the game."

"Whatever," Bird said, seemingly distracted, as though she hadn't really been listening. "Brandon is warming up. Come on. Let's go down there. I want to wish him luck. You can say something to Jason, make him feel better, maybe find out why everyone is giving him the cold shoulder."

She jumped up and started to climb over the bleachers to get to the field. I thought about staying and saving our places, but in the end, I grabbed my tote bag and followed her. Our seats would probably be empty when we got back, and if they weren't, we could find others.

By the time I got down there, Bird was standing to the left of the backstop, near the warm-up area, smiling at Brandon. It was obvious he was trying not to get caught smiling at her, that he was supposed to focus on the game.

I scooted over until I was standing behind the dugout. Jason was still messing with his gloves. I was surprised the Velcro still worked, that it hadn't worn down until all the tiny sticky teeth were gone.

"Hey, Jason," I said. "Awesome no-hitter."

I was vaguely aware of someone gasping and someone else moaning, as Jason came up off the bench fast, spun around, and stared at me like I'd morphed into something from *The X-Files*.

The guy who'd gasped, Chase, put one

knee on the bench, so he could talk to me in a low voice and still be heard. "You'd better go."

"Why? What did I do?"

"You never talk to the pitcher when . . ." He shook his head. "You just never talk to the pitcher when—"

"I just wanted to congratulate him on a good game—"

"It's not over 'til it's over," Chase said.

"You jinxed me," Jason said, crouching down in the corner, pressing his palms against his forehead, like he'd been struck with a migraine headache.

"You don't really believe that superstitious—"

His head came up so fast, and his stare was so hard that I stopped. He did believe. He really did believe. And judging by the way the other guys were looking at me, they all believed.

I backed away, not knowing what to say. I'd just felt sorry for him because he was being ignored. The guy at bat struck out, and Brandon was next. Bird had her fingers crossed while clutching the wire of the fence.

"I think I just made a big mistake," I said, my voice low.

"Yeah, I heard you. According to Brandon, you're never supposed to use the term *no-hitter* in the dugout."

"Well, I wasn't technically in the dugout."

"But your words traveled into the dugout. Close enough."

"Great. You don't really think I jinxed them, do you?"

Brandon struck out, the first time he'd struck out since playing for the Rattlers. When he walked by and glared at me, I found myself wishing Harry Potter was real, sitting in the stands, and could turn me into a rabbit's foot. I didn't really believe in bad luck. I believed we made our own luck, but I also understood the power of positive or negative thinking. If you think you'll lose, you'll lose.

The next inning, when six batters in a row got base hits off Jason, the coach put in a relief pitcher.

By that time, even people in the stands

were looking at me like it was my fault. Someone suggested I sit behind the dugout of the visiting team.

With that, I'd had enough. I located my dad at the top of the bleachers and asked him to take me home.

He did.

I knew Bird was having another pool party at her house following the game. I didn't know how much celebrating anyone might be doing, because I knew we'd lost. Dad and I had accessed the Rattler website, using his laptop so we could sit in the game room, and listened to the live broadcast.

I wasn't in the mood to go to Bird's party, even if I would have been welcomed. I had serious doubts I would be. And okay, I was chicken. I didn't want those doubts confirmed.

But I was in the mood for a party so I decided to throw one of my own—a pity party.

Wanting to soak in bubbles, I went into the bathroom. Tiffany had stretched mesh over the tub, so she could hand dry some of her clothes. Nothing of hers was wash-and-wear. It either had to be dry-cleaned or hand washed. Way too much trouble to move everything out of the way, as far as I was concerned. I had no idea where to put it all, and Tiffany would no doubt throw a fit, because I'd upset the drying process. She was a little particular about her clothes, and her hair, and her makeup.

I figured Jason wouldn't be home for a while, so I went into the bathroom across the hall. Seeing Jason's comb, shaving stuff, and hair trimmer, I felt like an intruder. Still, I knew I could do what I needed to do without messing anything up.

Opening the cabinet, I reached up to the top shelf and pulled out my box of pity party gear. I always used this bathroom when I needed total alone time.

I turned on the water and sprinkled in my passion peach bubble bath. While a glorious haven was being created, I set passion peach votive candles around the edge of the tub. I opened a bag of scented, dried peach blossoms and sprinkled them over the floor. I set an inflatable pillow at the head of the tub. When the bubbles were almost threatening to spill over the edge, I turned off the water, lit the candles, switched off the lights, removed my clothes, and climbed in. I sank beneath the silky, warm water until the bubbles were tickling my chin.

With the pillow tucked beneath my head, I thought, *I could go to sleep here.*

But it wasn't really sleep I wanted. I just wanted to feel pampered. I wanted to feel like I was doing something right. All I'd done was talk to a guy and he was horrified.

And to be honest, his reaction had stung. I'd wanted him to be happy to see me standing there. I'd wanted him to share something personal, like, "Did you see the way the batter just stared at the curveball when it went past?"

I'd wanted him to give me one of those slow grins, press his hand against mine for a high-five. I'd wanted—

The door clicked open. Jason stood there, staring at me. Why wasn't he at Bird's party? What was he doing here, and what exactly could he see in the shadowy bathroom?

I didn't dare move, didn't risk popping any bubbles.

"What are you doing in my bathroom?" he asked.

"I confused the left side of the hallway with the right?"

He looked like he wanted to say something else. Instead he just closed the door.

Sinking completely beneath the bubbles, I was determined to stay there forever.

Of course, I couldn't stay there forever. Eventually I needed to breathe, and more importantly, the bubbles began to disappear and the water started to get cold.

I got out of the tub, wrapped a big, thick towel around myself, gathered up my clothes, opened the door to the hallway, and peered out cautiously. Empty. Thank goodness.

I tiptoed across the floor to my room, not certain why I felt a need to tiptoe, but it just seemed like something I should do.

I thought about getting ready for bed, but whatever relaxation had taken place as I'd been in the tub had immediately left when Jason opened the door. I was tenser now than I had been at the game.

I put on a pair of old gym shorts and a soft, worn T-shirt that had BASEBALL = LIFE written across the front.

Then I went back across the hall to Jason's room. The door was open, but he wasn't inside. I glanced across the hallway. Tiffany's door was closed. She was probably already getting her beauty sleep.

I needed some chocolate chip cookie dough.

All the lights were turned off as I went downstairs, but Dad had plugged little indigo night lights into almost every wall socket, so he wouldn't have to turn on lights and disturb people when he got up in the middle of the night. Dad was a really light sleeper.

I crept into the kitchen, opened the freezer door, and groaned. Not a single pint of chocolate chip to be found. How had that happened?

I closed the door. Then I noticed the light over the back deck was spilling in through the windows into the kitchen. Talking to Dad was just what I needed. Maybe he could explain why baseball players seemed to be so obsessive-compulsive. It was like being trapped in a *Monk* episode.

I opened the back door and stepped outside . . .

Only it wasn't Dad on the porch. It was Jason, sitting in the lounge chair. I was sorta caught between a rock and a hard place. I didn't particularly want to move forward, because I didn't want him to think I'd come looking for him, but I didn't want to retreat, either. After all, this was my house, my turf. So I chose to get snappish. "Did you eat my ice cream?"

He was studying me like maybe I was insane. He lifted a brown bottle to his lips. Root beer. Then he finally shook his head. "No."

Okay, now was the time to leave. Instead I stepped outside, closed the door behind me, and dropped into the chair next to his.

"Look—" I began.

"Listen—" he said.

We looked at each other.

"You first," we said at the same time.

Then we both smiled, looked away. This

was awkward. Weird even. I was mad at him for ruining my evening, my enjoyment of the game. I supposed he was mad at me for ruining his pitching.

"Seriously," he said. "You first."

Originally I'd planned to apologize for laying some bad mojo on him or whatever he thought my talking to him had accomplished, but to do that would give the impression that I believed it had been my fault that his no-hitter streak had come to a crashing halt. And no way was it my fault. So I moved to neutral territory. "Why didn't you go to Bird's party?"

He took another sip of his root beer. "Didn't feel like partying."

"But you felt like moping around because a couple of guys got hits off you—"

"A couple? How 'bout six?"

"So what happened? You were really pitching tight. You were on fire—"

He shifted around in his chair so quickly that my breath backed up. "You talked to me."

"Do you know how stupid that sounds?"

"You don't understand." He got up and walked to the edge of the deck.

"Clearly I don't. No one was talking to you and you looked so lonely sitting in that corner alone. . . ."

He kept his back to me, but started shaking his head. "You don't talk to the pitcher when he's pitching a no-hitter. Everyone knows that. Baseball players are superstitious."

"Yeah, I get that. That's the reason Brandon touches every corner of home plate before each swing. It's the reason you unfasten and fasten your batting gloves. And you were pitching a no-hitter. I talked to you and now every guy is hitting off you." I came to my feet. "And it's all *my* fault. It's not that maybe four innings is too many to pitch. It's not that your arm got tired. It's because I talked to you. I brought you bad luck. Do you really believe that?"

He turned his head slightly and looked at me. I didn't realize how close I'd moved to him until he twisted around like that. When I'm angry, my ability to think seems to lock down; I'm pure emotion. And I was pretty angry, peeved I was being blamed for something that so wasn't my fault.

"I really believe it," he said quietly.

And just like that, I wasn't angry at him anymore. I was upset at myself, because no matter how unintentional, I'd ruined his night. If I knew him better, I'd have known to stay in the stands. I'd have known to stay away. And if he knew me better, maybe he'd understand why I'd done what I'd done.

"I'm sorry. I know how much players have to focus, and I know not to be a distraction. I just got caught up in the moment, in the great game, in your terrific pitching."

But I felt a need to explain more.

"Look, Jason, I love baseball. I love the crack of the bat hitting the ball. I love the seventh-inning stretch and singing 'Take Me Out to the Ball Game.' I love eating hot dogs and standing for the singing of the national anthem. I love doing the wave. I love Kiss Cam. I love that the game isn't over until it's over.

"I love the thrill of a home run and the disappointment of an out at first. I love the way a batter stands at the plate and the catcher readies himself to receive the pitch. I love watching the pitcher windup. I love sitting in the stands and feeling like I'm part of the game.

"And tonight, watching you pitch, I forgot that I'm only a small part—the spectator. Watching you, I felt like I was *in* the game, out on that field with you. You're out there on the mound, living a dream that so few people ever experience.

"I'm sorry, sorry that tonight I ruined the moment for you."

He was staring at me intently. I'd just bared my soul. Why didn't he speak? What could he possibly be thinking?

My nerves stretched taut.

"Say something," I demanded.

"There's nothing else to say," he said in that quiet way he had.

Then he lowered his head and kissed me.

Chapter 16

The way he was delivering that kiss—slowly, so amazingly slowly, like savoring the first pitch of the night, or your first time at bat, or your first home run, or your team playing in the World Series—I knew I could safely say he was no longer angry with me.

Wow!

That's all I was thinking when we finally came up for air about two minutes later.

"I shouldn't have done that," Jason said. "I really, really shouldn't have done that."

Okay. *Wow* obviously wasn't what was going through *his* mind.

The most disappointing thing of all? I knew he was right.

I just stood there nodding, not sure if I was

nodding yes, it should have happened, or yes, you're right, it shouldn't have happened.

He took a step back. "Let's just forget it, pretend it didn't happen, because it could make things really awkward, living in the same house and everything."

I started nodding faster. My throat felt like it was closing up. I wasn't going to cry, was I? I never cried.

He took another step back, waved his hand between us. "You and Mac . . ."

My head was going so fast now that my voice warbled. Or maybe it was my throat knotting. "Yeah, me and Mac . . ."

"Okay, then. This didn't happen."

"Right."

"'Night."

He disappeared into the house, leaving me on the back deck thinking that for something that didn't happen, it sure had felt real.

By the next evening, I could almost think about something other than Jason's kiss.

I hadn't told Bird about him kissing me. I was afraid that if I voiced what had happened out loud, Mom would somehow find out. And I didn't want her to send Jason packing.

So I just kept it all inside and tried to forget it. I tried to concentrate on getting ready for my "date."

Looking in the bathroom mirror, I was grateful to see that the knot was gone. The bruises were fading. I probably should have asked Tiffany to do her magic, but I just wasn't up to dealing with the bubbly that was usually Tiffany.

I parted my hair on the left side and swept it down over the bruise. No matter how many curling irons I heated, my hair refused to fluff for me. So be it. We were going to be outside, and the heat would no doubt cause it to droop, anyway.

I was really careful applying the mascara, keeping my eyes wide open until it dried—no clown spots this evening. I wriggled into my hip-hugging jeans and slipped on a lacy light blue camisole. I accessorized with a navy blue lace choker. Maybe I was half a Tiffany.

The doorbell rang. I closed my eyes and took a deep breath. My first official date with a guy from the baseball team. Shouldn't I have been more nervous? Or at least a little more excited? Mac was hot. He was cute. He was interested.

This was going to be fun.

And at the end of the evening, maybe he'd give me a kiss to make me forget all about Jason's.

I grabbed my big beach tote, the one I used when I was going anywhere near the water. I'd stuffed an old frayed quilt into it, because the outdoor amphitheater wasn't exactly set up for plush seating. Bird and I had been regulars last summer, and we pretty much had our routine down.

I stepped into the hallway at the same time that Jason was coming out of his room. He was wearing jeans and a burgundy T-shirt that accentuated his dark coloring. It was the first time I'd seen him since last night. He'd been noticeably absent all day, working I guess. Or practicing. Or maybe just avoiding me.

"Hey," I said.

"Hey."

I pointed to the stairs. "I'm going to the concert."

"Actually, Tiffany and I are going, too."

"Oh, really? You mean like a date?"

"No." He furrowed his brow, shook his head. "Just . . . friends I guess. She asked if I was doing anything tonight, and I wasn't, so . . ."

"That's good. You'll have fun. I'm glad. Really glad."

Okay, since I'd started running at the mouth, I decided to run for the stairs.

"Mac's really looking forward to tonight," Jason said.

I glanced over my shoulder and smiled so brightly I thought my jaw might come unhinged. "Me, too. I was kinda worried he wouldn't show, after my jinxing the team."

"You only jinxed me. I've been thinking about it all day. I realized that I overreacted."

"Ya *think*?"

"I'm trying to say I'm sorry."

"We decided last night didn't happen, so as far as I'm concerned, *all* of it didn't happen."

"Works for me."

"Excellent."

"Good deal."

"All right then."

I waited a beat. "We're on the same page."

"Absolutely."

We both grinned.

"I've run out of affirmatives," I said.

"Me, too."

"Okay, then."

Before we could start another volley of senseless banter, we both turned to the stairs. Partway down them, I heard voices. I wasn't rushing down the steps and had no plans to go swinging around the corner. As I neared the foyer, though, I heard Tiffany.

"But aren't all baseball players catchers? I mean, aren't they all supposed to catch the ball, so technically they're all catchers?"

I shook my head. She did *not* just ask that. No way.

But when I came around the corner, Mac was looking at her like she was an alien life-form. Maybe she was, because no one could be that ignorant.

Tiffany laughed. "I'm just teasing."

"That was a good one," Mac said, but he said it like maybe he thought it was as lame as I did.

Then he looked past her to me. "Hey, Dani."

"Hi."

He nodded at Jason, Jason nodded back, a real macho guy kinda greeting.

"I think we should all ride to the concert together," Tiffany announced.

Mac actually looked embarrassed. "Uh, I have a pickup truck, one front seat."

"Jason could drive, couldn't you, Jason?" she asked.

I wanted to say no, but I didn't know how to do it without sounding rude, and it looked like Jason didn't know how to, either, so we all ended up in his car.

"No misbehaving back there," Tiffany said from the passenger seat, with a totally fake-sounding giggle.

For a brief moment, I wondered if she was nervous. It was the kind of sound people make when they're nervous. But no way was she not feeling comfortable. I mean, she was accustomed to being on a stage, strutting her stuff in front of hundreds of people. And she had, like, a million dates, so going out with guys was no big deal for her.

While for me, it was an incredibly big deal.

I was sitting behind Jason, so I could see his eyes in the rearview mirror. He was so serious, like driving down this street took immense concentration.

"This is going to be so much fun," Tiffany said. "We can all sit together at the concert."

"We're meeting Bird there," I told her.

"She can sit with us, too," Tiffany said, like she was being really generous in making room for my friend.

"Actually, it'll be Bird and Brandon."

She twisted around slightly. "Who's Brandon?"

"One of the other baseball players in town for the summer."

"That'll be fun to include him, too. I bet the guys know him."

Jason and Mac kinda grunted, which I figured was their way of telling her she'd guessed correctly.

"I'll see. Bird may have other plans." I didn't want to commit Bird to sitting with us if she didn't want to. Besides, I wasn't totally certain I wanted to sit anywhere near Jason. It would be more than weird after what happened last night. Between trying to forget him and trying to impress Mac, my nerves were definitely on edge. Add Tiffany to the mix, and I could see only disaster on the horizon. I just wasn't certain how many of her silly comments I'd have patience for tonight.

I glanced over at Mac and really wished I hadn't, because his gaze was focused on Tiffany, or as much of her as he could see, considering he was sitting right behind her. Tiffany with her hair all flowing around her, her makeup all perfect, and her shoulders bare because she was wearing a halter top.

My tolerance for silly comments was going to be zero.

When we got to the amphitheater, we did end up all sitting together on the grassy knoll. Brandon, Bird, me, Mac, Tiffany, and Jason. In that order.

The stage was set up at the bottom of a small hill and the seats were carved into the landscape, reinforced with stonework, so it looked like a series of wide steps. People sat on the steps. Except at the very top—which was where we were—they sat on blankets.

The band was local. The Blue Moon Group. The music had a dark, edgy sound to it. I couldn't really decipher the lyrics, since they were screamed more than sung. It wasn't the type of show I'd expected, but the concert committee had advertised they'd have an assortment of bands, orchestras, and offerings throughout the summer. This group had this whole Goth thing going, with leather and chains.

"This music is so un-Ragland. Do you think the committee thought they were booking Blue *Man* Group?" Bird asked, near my ear, loudly.

There weren't any people sitting near us to be disturbed, and the volume of the music actually had the ground shaking. I wondered if they could cause an earthquake. Not that we were prone to earthquakes. Tornadoes were more our speed.

My answer to Bird's question was just a shrug. I was trying not to feel like a third wheel. Or in this case, a fifth wheel. Honestly, it was like I'd come without a date.

"How does she do that?" Bird asked.

I didn't have to ask who the *she* was. I knew it was Tiffany. Nor did I have to ask what Bird was referring to. Jason and Mac were leaning toward Tiffany, listening to whatever it was she was saying, like it was the most interesting thing in the world.

"Does she wear, like, turn-'em-stupid perfume or something?" Bird asked.

"I don't know. Maybe guys like thinking they're way smarter than girls."

"It's gotta be an act. No one is that brainless." She grimaced. "I don't mean to dis your sister, but really, does anyone think the moon actually turns blue?"

Yeah, Tiffany had asked, "So when does the moon turn blue?"

Mac had laughed and explained that a blue moon was the second full moon in a month, that a full moon appeared every twenty-nine nights, and so it was truly rare to have two full moons in any given month. He'd said he'd taken a class in astronomy.

"Oh, I love astronomy. I'm a Pisces. What sign are you?"

Which had made Mac laugh again, and he started to explain the difference between astronomy and astrology. Tiffany was apparently absolutely fascinated . . . and fascinating. His gaze—and Jason's—was riveted on her.

I gave another little shrug, feeling a need to defend my sister, who might be in need of a trip down the yellow brick road to ask the wizard for some brains. "I wasn't exactly sure what a blue moon was, either."

"But you know the difference between astronomy and astrology."

"Let's just enjoy the concert, okay?"

Which would have been a lot easier to do if halfway through it, Bird and Brandon didn't start a kiss fest. Not that I could blame them. Music, crickets chirping, stars coming out as night descended . . . it was romantic.

Brandon had definitely gotten to first base with Bird, while I hadn't even gotten up to the plate with Mac. I couldn't say the same about Jason. We had gotten to first base, but then it was like the umpire had yelled, "Foul ball!"

Mac touched my shoulder. Finally, I thought, finally we're going to start getting to know each other. We're going to talk. He's going to be interested in me, and I'll be interested in him.

"Your sister and I are going to the concession stand. Want anything?"

A date? A boyfriend? A guy kissing me?

"No thanks."

"I'll be right back."

I watched as he and Tiffany made their way down the slope to the steps. He had his hand resting on the small of her back, supposedly to help keep her balanced so she didn't take a tumble. Part of me thought I should see that as a plus in his favor. A considerate guy. Maybe I'd feel better about it if his hand was on my back.

"Did she just steal your date?" Bird asked, clearly incensed enough to take a break from kissing Brandon.

"They're just going to get something to drink."

"They better be. Otherwise, I'll short-sheet his bed."

I felt movement to my right. Jason had slid over, so he was now sharing my blanket. Part of me wished he hadn't kissed me last night, because before that moment—that incredible moment—we'd become really comfortable around each other, and now we were back to that awkwardness. But part of me, a larger part of me, wished he'd kiss me again.

Even if he had thought it was a mistake. As far as mistakes went, it was one of the best ones I'd ever experienced.

He moved in so our cheeks were almost touching, his mouth near mine, so we could talk without having to shout.

"Interesting band," he said.

"Understatement of the summer."

"You know any of the members?"

"Why? Do you want to meet them?"

"Not really. Just making conversation. Thought maybe since they were local . . ."

"I think maybe they're using aliases. I mean, do you think a mom actually named her kid Vegas?"

He tipped his head toward Bird.

"That's not her real name."

"So maybe a mom nicknamed her kid Vegas."

"Maybe. But I think they're using stage names."

"I would if I were them."

"You don't like the music?"

He shrugged. "I'm more of a Faith Hill fan."

"Yeah, I'd rather listen to Green Day."

He nodded.

I didn't know what to say, where to take the conversation from there, so I said something that probably was really none of my business. "You didn't want anything from the concession stand?"

"Three's a crowd."

I nodded in sympathy and understanding. "Yeah, Mac and Tiffany really seemed to hit it off."

He nodded. "Yeah, I've been a little surprised to see his attention . . . wander."

"That's a nice way to put it."

"It's hard being in a town where you know so few people. Think he's just trying to make friends. We all are."

"Friends, huh?"

"Yeah. We're not staying, Dani. We're here

for a couple of months, playing ball, having some kicks where we can."

"And last night."

"Was a mistake. I told you that."

But I think I was hoping, after sleeping on it, he might have changed his mind.

"Looks like Brandon's heading toward second base with your friend," he said, in one of his now familiar let's-change-the-subject-tactics.

Heavy petting. Bird and I had researched the dating definitions on the Internet, because we figured baseball players would talk in baseball terms when dating, and we certainly didn't want to give a guy the impression he was going to hit a home run with us if he wasn't.

"Bird really likes him," I said.

"He's a good guy."

"I don't mean to question your judgment, but you said Mac was a good guy, too, but I'm not seeing that."

"Give him a chance."

I wondered if Mac was going to give Tiffany a chance, if I was the favorite only when beautiful Tiffany wasn't around.

"Can I ask you a question?" I asked after a few minutes.

"Sure."

"I've always wondered . . . what exactly *do* a catcher and pitcher discuss at the mound?"

He studied me for a second, before finally saying, "Last night we talked about you."

Chapter 17

I was stunned.

"You talked about me? Was this before or after I talked to you in the dugout?"

"Before."

"What? Why? What was there to say?"

"Okay, you two, make room for us," Tiffany said, returning from the concession stand, handing Jason a bottled water and nudging him back over to the blanket they were sharing.

What could they have possibly been saying about me?

Mac sat beside me. "I know you said you didn't want anything, but since I was down there . . ."

"Thanks." Forcing myself to smile, to not

start grilling him about the conversation at the mound, I took the bottle of water he offered.

He leaned toward me. "Your sister's funny."

"Oh, yeah, she's a regular Rita Rudner."

"She said she's never been to a baseball game. That's un-American."

He sounded genuinely appalled.

"She keeps busy with other things."

"So she was saying. Man, I had no idea that beauty queens worked so hard."

"She's not really a queen."

"She wears a crown."

"Technically, I think it's a tiara."

"So what is she, a princess?"

She did have a T-shirt with silver rhinestones on it spelling out PRINCESS.

"I suppose." Ready to move on.

He took my hand. Actually took my hand. I waited for the spark I felt every time Jason touched me, but nothing happened. I mean, Mac had a nice hand. Warm. A little rough on the surface. I liked holding his hand. It almost made me forget about the feel of Jason's.

Mac grinned. "Okay, we've covered the

free and the cheap. What else is there to do in this town?"

For the remainder of the concert, his attention was on me. We talked about a lot of things. His major—business. His kid sister—he was planning to go home the next weekend because it was her birthday. His divorced parents—he hated being a statistic. His dream to play in the majors—for his hometown Astros.

"You know the worst part about a date?" he finally asked.

"Realizing it was a mistake?"

He laughed, then sobered. "Is that what you think this one is?"

"Oh, no, not at all." But I couldn't help but wonder if maybe he did.

"Good. Anyway, the worst part? Worrying about the good-night kiss. Puts a lot of pressure on a guy . . . building up to that moment. Who needs it? You know?"

I didn't know what to say. I was a little disappointed. First official date. No kiss. "I never thought about it like that."

"But I have a solution, to eliminate the pressure."

"Oh, yeah?"

"Yeah. Let's just get it over with."

And he kissed me.

It was my first public, in front of a thousand people—so, okay, maybe there were only two hundred at the concert—kiss. It had grown dark, and I really, really hoped Jason wasn't able to see this, that he wasn't on the other side of Tiffany saying, "Looks like Mac is heading to first base with your sister."

Last night, he and I were kissing, and now I felt self-conscious that less than twenty-four hours later I was kissing someone else. Kissing someone else who was attempting to "get it over with."

Not exactly a move I'd score a ten on the romantic scale.

Even though the kiss itself was worthy of a ten. Well, maybe an eight, because all kinds of doubts kept flashing through my mind. Did he *want* to be pressing his mouth to mine? Was this an obligation kiss? Or was he just nervous, worrying about the end of the date?

And what was Tiffany thinking? It was a toss-up as to which was worse: kissing in front of her or kissing in front of Jason.

Mac drew back. Even in the darkness, I could see the white of his grin. "No more pressure."

He took my hand and leaned forward as though he wanted to listen more intently to the concert. Unfortunately, it gave me a clear view of Jason who was, yep, looking in my direction.

I felt a need to apologize, which was silly. Mac was my date. He might even be more. He could be rounding first base to become my boyfriend.

It was a little after eleven when we got home. Tiffany and Jason went into the house, leaving me alone on the porch with my date.

"I had a good time," he said.

"Me, too."

"Maybe we can do it again."

"I'd like that."

"You know, I'm sorta regretting we went ahead and got the kiss over with. Ruined having anything to look forward to at the end of the date."

I grinned. "Yeah, that is a downside."

"Good night, then, with no good-night kiss."

"Good night."

He took a step off the porch. Turned back to me. "Can't do it," he said, and gave me another kiss. Then grinning broadly, like he was pleased with himself, he left.

When I walked inside, Mom was waiting in the foyer and said, "How was the concert?"

"Loud."

Tiffany and Jason were nowhere to be seen, so I assumed they'd headed on upstairs.

"Tiffany said it was fun."

"Did she say anything else?"

"Like what?"

I shrugged. That she'd watched me playing a game of tonsil hockey? "That it was loud?"

"Are you okay?"

"I'm fine. Don't suppose you replaced that missing carton of ice cream I left you a note about."

"Your dad did."

"Great."

I pulled the pint of chocolate chip cookie

dough ice cream out of the freezer, grabbed a spoon, and went upstairs. I was going to go to my room, but I noticed light flickering in the game room. The TV was on, the lights out, the French doors closed.

I peered through one of the panes and could see Jason sitting on the reclining love seat, his back to me, because the love seat was in the middle of the room, right in front of the TV.

I debated with myself: go to my room, join Jason in the game room.

I pushed on the door, and it made an audible click that could be heard even with the TV on. Jason glanced back over his shoulder.

"Can I come in?" I asked.

"Hey, it's your house, your TV, your TiVo."

Grinning, I stepped into the room and closed the door behind me. "Actually, everything you just named technically belongs to my parents."

I sat on the love seat, curled my feet beneath me, took the lid off the carton of ice cream, set it on the small glass-topped table beside me, and spooned out a bit with a nice ball of cookie dough in it.

I ate the ice cream and pointed my empty spoon toward the TV. "So you're a fan of *House*?"

He hit the TiVo's pause button just as a patient flat-lined. "I've only watched a few episodes. Not sure I'd want this guy to be my doctor."

I laughed. "I hear you. He seems to have a lot of wrong diagnoses. Dad actually has this irritating habit of hitting the button to see how much time is left whenever they come up with a diagnosis. If there's too much time left, he'll go, 'That's not it.' I'm not even sure why we like the show. It's not like the symptoms mean anything to us and we can figure out what's wrong with the patients."

"I think people like that House says out loud the things we all wish we could say."

And I wondered if he had things he wanted to say.

"Can I be honest?" I asked.

"Sure, but I already know what you're going to say. You like that guy who plays Chase."

I grinned, deciding not to admit it had been

weird kissing Mac in front of him. "When he talks, sure. I have a soft spot for accents. *TV Guide* named him one of the sexiest guys on TV, and if *TV Guide* says it, you know it's true. I'll bet you like Cameron."

He grinned back at me. "Cuddy."

"Ah. I think she's my dad's favorite, too, but don't tell Mom." I spooned out another bit of ice cream. "Sure you don't want any?"

He shrugged and leaned toward me. "Okay, I'll take some."

Which I'd so not expected, and which had me wondering what I was supposed to do now. Stick my spoon in his mouth?

I felt a cold drip on the hand holding the carton and realized my spoon was suspended and the ice cream was starting to melt. I extended it toward him, watched as his mouth closed around my spoon. Now what? I was so not used to feeding guys.

He wrapped his hand around my wrist and guided my hand back. I watched appreciation glide over his face like hot fudge over a banana split.

"It tastes like you," he said.

The heat rushed into my face. "Uh, yeah, my lip balm . . . same flavor."

"I think it just became my favorite ice cream."

Ookaay. So was that an endorsement of my kiss?

"You say that like you'd never tried it before."

"I hadn't."

I stared at him. "It's one of their most famous. How could you not try it?"

"I'm not into trends. Just because someone else is doing it, doesn't mean I want to."

I glanced down at the ice cream melting in the carton. I remembered *his* taste—root beer. And Mac's? I really couldn't say.

It was rare when I didn't delve into ice cream with gusto. "Earlier you said you and Mac had talked about me. What exactly?"

"Just usual guy stuff."

"Like what?"

"How much he likes you."

My insecurities were circling. "Did he like me before Dave and Bubba's, before Tiffany put me through the extreme makeover?"

"Why wouldn't he?"

He sounded completely baffled, like maybe I'd just asked a Tiffany-style question.

"Okay, look, earlier, when I mentioned being honest, I just wanted to say that it was weird kissing Mac in front of you, because I don't kiss guys in front of people. So, anyway, I just wanted you to know that."

"Consider it known."

"Okay then."

I got up. "Do you want me to leave this with you?"

"Sure you don't mind?"

"Nah." I handed him the carton and spoon. "Enjoy."

My offer wasn't totally generous. I took perverse pleasure at the thought he'd think about me with each bite.

I wondered if maybe he might have been my date tonight if he wasn't living in my house.

Would it be rude to ask him to move out?

Chapter 18

It was official. I had a boyfriend.

Not that Mac or I used the BF/GF designation when referring to each other, but it was pretty obvious. We hung out together after practice and after the games. And we were doing a whole lot of kissing.

It was also obvious that whatever bad luck I'd brought the team had dissipated. We won three games in a row. The final game, against the Denton Outlaws, was a shutout. Jason pitched his best game ever.

I never saw him at Bird's parties, but then he'd been scarce lately. We still did our morning exercise routine. During one session, we'd brainstormed an idea I had for my column — the joys and trials of hosting a player and being hosted by a family you didn't know, adjusting to their routines. We'd tossed back and forth some of the different challenges. I was hoping to have an opportunity to actually interview him in more depth, as research for the article.

But like I said, he wasn't around much.

I found myself thinking about that recent development as I checked my e-mail Thursday morning.

One of the e-mails that popped up was marked with the subject "Appreciation Splash!" and was from owners@raglandrattlers.com. Beginning Sunday, the team had three days with no games. The team owners—yes, they actually had owners—had decided to thank the families for providing homes for the team players by having an appreciation day at The Splash Zone, one of the area water parks. Tickets were heavily discounted and a pavilion had been reserved for our use.

Of course, Bird called me about ten seconds after the e-mail hit my inbox to confirm that she and Brandon were definitely up for going. Did I think Mac and I would go?

"Actually, this is the weekend he's going

home for his sister's birthday," I told her.

"Oh, right," Bird said. "I forgot he'd mentioned that to my parents. So you want to go with us?"

"Probably not."

"Come on, Dani. We can still have fun. It's a family appreciation thing. You should be there. After all, you're the whole reason we're involved. Jason'll probably invite you anyway."

Would he? I wasn't so sure.

"But if he doesn't, you can go with us. Okay?"

"We'll see."

I left it at that, because now that I was used to being part of a pair, I didn't know if I really wanted to be a third wheel again.

A knock sounded on my door.

Okay, Mom and Dad were at work, so it wasn't them. And Tiffany didn't knock. She felt like walking into rooms was her right.

I set the phone on the nightstand, walked to the door, and opened it.

Jason was standing there, one hand in the back pocket of his jeans. "Hey."

"Hey."

The awkwardness between us was back. It came and went, with no obvious rhyme or reason.

Suddenly his eyes widened as he looked behind me. "Whoa! When you said you loved baseball"—he looked at me with new appreciation in his eyes—"you really do."

"I really do."

"It's like a museum."

"I prefer to think of it as a living scrapbook."

He pointed to the wall decorated with caps and pennants. "You collect caps?"

"Actually, I get the team caps every time Dad and I go to a game."

"You've seen all those teams play, in person?" He sounded completely awed.

I couldn't help but grin. "Yeah. You want to look at them? Come on in."

I watched as he slowly walked around my room, looking at all my displayed memorabilia. He stopped in front of a large framed collage of photos of Dad and me in front of various ballparks—Wrigley Field, Yankee Stadium, Fenway Park, Tiger Stadium, to name a few.

"You've actually watched games at these ballparks?" he asked.

"Yeah. Dad and I take a trip to a different ballpark each year. It's his dream to visit every one, and it's no fun to go alone."

"Some of these don't even exist anymore."

"Yeah, I know. But I once sat in their seats. Pretty cool, huh?"

"Absolutely."

He turned and looked at me. "The posters and pictures in my room, those are yours, aren't they?"

"On loan to the guest room while you're here. I thought you'd enjoy them."

"Immensely. Thanks. And speaking of thanks. The team is showing its appreciation to the host families by taking them to a water park on Sunday. I know Mac is going out of town, but I thought you might still want to go. I mean, not as a date or anything. I'm going to invite the whole family."

"You don't have to work Sunday?"

"I got scheduled off."

"Sounds like fun. We could pack a picnic lunch—"

"I'll take care of that. As *my* thank you. All you have to do is bring yourself."

"And a bathing suit."

He grinned. "Yeah, and a bathing suit."

"And a towel. And suntan lotion . . ."

"Maybe it'd be simpler if I just said I'll take care of the tickets and eats."

"Okay, but I'll go ahead and warn you not to take it personally that Mom and Dad aren't really into water parks. It's that whole not-using-the-exercise-equipment-as-intended thing Dad has going."

His grin grew. "I won't take it personally."

"Okay, then, Sunday."

As though suddenly realizing how intimate it seemed to be in my bedroom, he cleared his throat and took a step back.

He gave my room one more look and took another step back. "It's amazing what a room can reveal."

Then he walked down the hallway and knocked on Tiffany's door.

I wondered what he'd discover looking into her room.

* * *

Sunday afternoon Tiffany called shotgun and sat in the front seat with Jason.

When we got to the water park, Jason handed each of us a ticket and it occurred to me—since there was a dollar amount on it—that he might have paid for them.

"Do we owe you money for these?" I asked.

"Course not. It's my treat," he said as he lifted a cooler he'd borrowed from Dad out of the trunk.

"But you shouldn't have to pay for everything."

He looked at me like I'd suddenly turned into Tiffany. "But it's appreciation day. Of course I should pay for things."

"But—"

"Can we please go?" Tiffany asked. "It's really hot out here in the parking lot."

Like she didn't think it would be hot in the cemented water park.

As we trudged to the entrance, I decided I'd find a way to even out the whole paying-for-our-ticket situation. I'd go to Ruby Tuesday, sit at a table Jason was waiting on, and leave a really large tip. It wasn't fair for a starving baseball player to pay our way. Not that he was actually starving, but still.

A thousand people were lined up to get into the park, but apparently groups used a special entrance, and we had special tickets, so it didn't take us long to get inside. The team owners had provided a map of the water park, with the reserved pavilion clearly marked.

It was right in front of the wave pool, a pool that created gigantic waves for a while before settling into calmness. Right then it was in its calm stage. Several picnic tables were inside the pavilion. I wasn't surprised to see Bird waving from the table she'd claimed for us. Jason carried the cooler to the table.

"Hey, guys," Bird said while applying sunscreen to her legs.

I'd applied plenty before I left the house, wanting to give it time to soak in.

"Thought we'd head to the Bubba Tub first, while we're all together," she said.

"Not me," Tiffany said. "I don't actually do the water. I'm just going to lay out by the pool." She took her towel out of her beach bag. "See you later."

Bird had lowered her sunglasses, so she had a clearer view of Tiffany walking away. "She comes to a water park but doesn't actually *do* the water? What's up with that?"

"Don't try to figure her out," I said. "There is no Tiffany Code."

"That would make an interesting movie," she said. Then shook her head. "No, I guess it wouldn't. So? Bubba Tub? It's a four-person ride."

Okay, this was more than awkward, because since only four of us were standing by the table, it sounded like her invitation was for everyone, which included Jason, and yet I now had a boyfriend, but I sure didn't want to do the rides alone . . .

"I'm good with that," Jason said. Nothing suggestive in his tone. Nothing possessive. Nothing other than *let's just have a great time.*

"Yeah, sure, let's do it," I said.

I slipped off my flip-flops and removed the T-shirt I'd been wearing over my white bandeau bikini. And yes, for a second there, I thought I had the attention of both guys, but it was hard to be sure since they were wearing sunglasses.

Brandon cleared his throat and held up his wrist. A key was dangling from a corded bracelet. "I rented a locker over here if anyone wants to put away their valuables."

"Yeah, let me put my wallet and keys in there," Jason said.

"Nothing for me, thanks," I said.

The guys walked off together to see to manly things.

"It's a shame Mac went home this weekend," Bird said, putting the cap on her suntan lotion and dropping it in her tote bag.

"Yeah," I said, trying hard to miss him. Should I have to try? "But it was nice of him to want to be with his sister."

"Definitely. He's a nice guy. So you really like him, huh?"

"Sure."

Bird looked at me over her sunglasses, exactly as she'd looked at Tiffany. It made me squirm and want to explain.

"We just do a lot of kissing and not much else."

"You mean like, you're not heading to second base."

"No, I mean, we don't really talk about anything. We don't share interests. It's hard to explain. It's just, I'm not as happy as I thought I'd be once I got a boyfriend."

"So maybe you have the wrong boyfriend."

Before I could comment on that, Jason and Brandon joined us, and we headed for the Bubba Tub. I hadn't considered how awkward it would be walking to a ride with another couple, a couple obviously in serious *like* mode. Brandon had his arm around Bird, she was snuggled up against his side. Jason and I were walking side by side with our arms dangling loosely. At one point our fingers touched, and I think we both jumped, sensing the forbidden current.

"So, do you come here often?" Jason finally asked.

"A couple of times each summer. Not often enough to get a season pass." I shrugged. "I mean, there are so many water parks in the area, why limit options?"

He grinned. "I hear you."

He was, of course, wearing only his swim trunks, having removed his T-shirt as well. He was really fit and trim, a little more tanned than I expected, so I figured he must have been playing ball occasionally without his shirt on. Maybe all the guys did, because Brandon was tanned, too.

We got to the Bubba Tub and started climbing the steps to the top where we'd get in the tub and ride it down the winding slope. Of course, the long line made the going slow. Maybe this was the reason Tiffany didn't do water, because it involved a lot of standing around, trying to think up a conversation. Of course, Brandon and Bird were using the time to kiss.

"Seen any good movies lately?" I asked, just to have something to say.

Jason laughed, like he knew exactly what I was trying to do. Fill the dead air between us.

"Not really. So why do you think we go through this?"

"Through what?"

"Waiting in these long lines for what will probably be a thirty-second thrill."

"I guess we figure a thirty-second thrill is better than no thrill at all."

"So what's your favorite ride?"

"I have two actually. Avalanche and the Lazy River."

"What's Avalanche?"

"The tallest, fastest . . . it's almost a straight drop, on your back, arms crossed." I shuddered. "It's really a rush, no pun intended."

"I'll have to try it."

"We could do it after this one," I said, before I could stop myself, before I convinced myself that out of loyalty to Mac, I should spend the day riding alone.

"Okay," Jason said.

He seemed slightly amused, but it was difficult to be sure because he was wearing sunglasses. Of course, so was I.

Jason leaned down and said, his voice low, "Look, I know you're with Mac. But who wants to be at a water park alone? Let's just have fun."

I smiled at him. "I like your thinking."

We finally got to the top and climbed into the huge inner tube, boy, boy, girl, girl, so Bird and I were sitting beside each other with Brandon beside her and Jason beside him. We grabbed the straps along the bottom of the tube.

Brandon and Jason were wearing huge grins.

"You realize our side is weighted more than yours," Brandon said.

"Yeah, so?" Bird said.

"So we're going to go fast," he said, just as an attendant pushed the tube over the edge.

Bird and I screamed and laughed most of the way down, while the guys just laughed. I'd never been to a water park with a guy, and it was fun, really fun, riding this ride with the guys.

"Let's do the Black Void next," Bird said, as we climbed out of the tube at the bottom of the slope.

"We were thinking Avalanche," I said.

"Yeah, but the Black Void is right here, and Avalanche is on the other side of the park."

I looked at Jason. He grinned, shrugged. "Black Void is fine with me."

I wondered if he realized the Black Void

was a two-person ride. I thought about asking who was going to ride with whom, but since Bird was already nestled against Brandon's side, it seemed like a pointless question.

"Black Void it is," I said. Not willing to admit that I wasn't entirely disappointed I would be riding it with Jason.

It was a five-hundred-foot tunnel. The inner tube was designed for two-person seating. I sat in the front with my legs stretched out over the tube. Jason was in the sitting area behind me, his legs along the side. I had to lean back a little, which put my back against his chest. I guess he could have held on to the sides of the tube. Instead, his arms came around me.

"Okay?" he asked, his voice low near my ear.

"Yeah." I sounded breathless. I'm sure it was the anticipation of the ride, not his nearness.

A red light at the top of the tunnel switched to green, someone pushed us, and then we were plunging into the black abyss.

"Awesome!" Jason said as we came out from the ride, holding hands.

I'm not sure either of us had given the taking of hands any real thought. It just seemed like the thing you should do after traveling through the darkness to the final splash.

"That was totally cool," Jason said.

"Totally," I said.

Bird and Brandon came out next, Brandon wearing a grin wide enough to challenge Jason's.

"Where to next?" Brandon asked.

"Avalanche?" I suggested.

"Let's go."

"I think I could go to sleep right here," Jason said.

It was late afternoon. The four of us were in individual inner tubes, floating along the Lazy River, which was basically a narrow, three-foot pool that circled the entire park, the water somehow set up so it flowed constantly and slowly.

Jason and I were holding hands so our tubes didn't wander away from each other. I think we'd ridden every slide and tube the park had to offer. We'd gone back to the pavilion to eat lunch. Jason had brought ham sandwiches, which I recognized as coming from Ruby Tuesday. Brandon had brought drinks and chips. Apparently they'd coordinated their food efforts. I guess they'd figured we'd be hanging out together.

Tiffany had taken a pass on eating. She was entertaining a couple of guys in the pool area. By entertaining, I mean asking silly questions they were dumb enough to try to answer.

Now we were letting our food settle, before taking another shot at the rides we'd enjoyed most.

"I know after all the thrill rides that it seems strange to enjoy this ride, but I love having a few moments of calm," I said.

"Nah, I like it, too," Jason said.

His fingers squeezed mine. "I wasn't sure you'd hang out with me today."

I looked over at him, glad I was wearing sunglasses so he couldn't read whatever expression might be in my eyes. "I'm family, right?"

"Right."

I lifted our hands, splashed them in the

water. "I had fun. I'm glad you invited me."

"I'm glad you came."

Okay, could we get any more lame? It's like we were both trying to say something without saying anything.

I swallowed hard. "What would you have done if Tiffany 'did water'?"

"You mean if I'd had to choose who to ride the rides with?"

"Yeah."

"It could have gotten awkward."

"Yeah."

"You're more fun," he said.

I almost said, "You are, too." But that would have been totally unfair to Mac. For all I knew he was a blast at a water park.

I heard the rush of the waterfall, and unhooked my fingers from Jason's. The river had this spot where water cascaded in various sheets, but if you guided your tube just right, you could slip through an open space, so you didn't get hit. I began to maneuver to the side.

As I neared the falls, I felt a tug on my tube and looked back. Jason had his hand on it and was grinning broadly.

"No way are you not going through the falls," he said.

"I don't like them."

"You don't 'do' water?"

"I don't 'do' waterfalls."

"Oh, yeah, you do."

With me kicking and screaming, he pushed me off my course and sent me through the falls. I purposely dumped myself over on the other side and was standing, waiting, when he came through. I put my hands beneath his tube and dumped him over.

"Hey!" he yelled before he went under.

I was laughing as I plowed through the water to snag my inner tube. I hoisted myself on it, smiling as I watched him threading through the water, dragging his tube behind him to catch up with me.

"You don't want to mess with me," I warned, unable to stop my grin.

"No, I guess I don't." He climbed into his tube, leaned back, and took my hand.

"You're really fun to be with, Dani," Jason said.

It almost sounded like he was saying something else. Something deeper, more intense. Something you didn't say to a girl who had a boyfriend.

We stayed until the park closed at eight. I called shotgun, so I sat in the front on the way home.

But it was like the water park had been a magical place where Jason and I could laugh, have fun, hold hands. But it wasn't real.

The magic disappeared as soon as we walked out through the gate.

Chapter 19

"What *are* they talking about?" Bird asked. "I've never seen a pitcher and catcher spend so much time on the mound. This is, what, the third time this inning?"

Since it was Jason and Mac, I wondered if they were talking about me again. And maybe I didn't really want to know what they were saying.

Mac had returned to Ragland late that afternoon, just in time for the big Rattlers pre-tailgate party my dad had thrown in our back-yard, early enough that the players could join us before the game and grab a couple of the burgers he was grilling.

I was glad to see Mac, but feeling guilty, too. I couldn't forget how much fun I'd had with Jason at the water park, the feel of his hand in mine, the way he'd looked so triumphant and pleased when he'd pushed me beneath the falls. I couldn't forget the appreciation and awe in his voice as he'd walked through my bedroom and looked at all the things that were important to me. And I knew — *knew!* — that if I invited Mac to see my room, he'd think I was offering another kind of invitation.

Mac didn't know me the way Jason did. But he was my boyfriend. Wasn't he?

But if he was, why had I spotted him giving Tiffany miniature golf pointers at Dad's party? His arms wrapped around her, his hands on hers as they gripped the golf club. It was way too similar to our encounter at Dave and Bubba's.

But what really bothered me was that I wasn't upset. Shouldn't I have been upset?

Put Tiffany in the front seat of the car with Jason, and I'd be trying not to go ballistic because she was that close to him.

Mac and Jason were obviously disagreeing about something. Both of them being on the mound made no sense. Jason was pitching an almost-perfect game.

The umpire shouted at them. Mac shook his head and trudged back to the plate. Jason did his pre-pitch warm-up. Then he threw the ball with such force that the *thwump* it made when it hit Mac's glove was louder than usual.

"Strike three! You're out!" the umpire yelled.

It was the third out of the second inning. The Rattlers were heading to the dugout. When Mac got close to Jason, he shoved Jason's shoulder. Jason shoved back. Mac took a swing—

Jason lunged for him.

The crowd jumped to its feet and started yelling, but it was like, who did we yell for? Because these were the kind of cheap shots you saw players on opposing teams make.

These guys played on the same team!

The coaches ran onto the field, while the umpire pulled them apart. Then the coaches yelled at them. One led them back to the dugout, yammering at them as they went. The umpire and the head coach talked.

The head coach went back to the dugout while the umpire yelled, "Play ball!"

"What was *that* about?" Bird asked as we took our seats. "I've never seen anything like it before."

I could only shake my head. No way could it have been about me. Could it?

The after-game party at Bird's was subdued. We'd won. Everyone should have been celebrating, but tension abounded. Jason was nowhere to be seen.

If anyone knew what had caused the friction on the field, no one was saying. Not even Mac.

We were sitting on the edge of the pool, our bare feet dangling in the water. It was the first time since the concert that kissing didn't seem to be on his mind.

As a matter of fact, all he did was sit and sigh. And in typical fashion, I couldn't think of anything to say to him, because I figured any topic I offered, he wouldn't want to talk about. But finally, I got up the courage and asked, "What was going on between you and Jason?"

"Let's just drop it, okay?"

"We haven't really picked it up."

"And we're not going to."

"Okay, then, how about this? At Dad's pre-tailgate party, while I went to get us drinks, you went to give Tiffany golfing pointers. What's up with that?"

"Her ball kept missing the hole, that's all. So I thought I'd help her out. No big deal."

My insecurities ratcheted up a notch. "She's really pretty."

"Yeah." He sounded distracted.

"Do you wish she was here?"

"Why do girls always blow things out of proportion? I had a five-hour drive from Houston. I should have come back yesterday. I'm gonna call it a night."

He kissed me on the cheek, got up, and walked off.

Ooookay.

Since I'd ridden over with him—in silence—I was without transport home.

Bird sat beside me. "So, did he tell you what was going on?"

"Nope."

"Weird."

"Weirder yet, he's going to bed, and I don't have a ride home."

"I'll take you. This party is the most boring one we've ever had."

Five minutes later, I was walking through my front door. The house was dark, but I could see faint light coming from the kitchen. I figured maybe it was Dad, still up, waiting for me.

Only it was Jason in the dimly lit room, sitting at the table wearing a T-shirt with the sleeves cut off. He had a huge ice pack wrapped around his left shoulder.

"Ohmigod! Did Mac hurt you that bad?" I asked, coming farther into the kitchen. Jason had pitched two more innings after their encounter.

"He didn't hurt me at all. Sometimes I need to ice down my shoulder after I pitch, that's all."

"Is it hurting?"

"It'll be okay."

Which wasn't an acknowledgment or a denial.

"Is there something I can do?" *Like kiss it*

and make it better? As if I'd ever say that out loud. But I hated the thought of him in pain.

"No."

His left elbow was resting on the table. His fingers, curled around a small bowl, were soaking in—I sniffed the zesty aroma—"Is that pickle juice?"

Jason grinned. "Yeah. It toughens the skin, helps prevent blisters."

"I've never heard of that."

"Your dad has." He pointed to a large pickle jar on the counter. "He brings the jars home from the concession stand when all the pickles are sold, so I'll have plenty of brine."

I pulled out a chair and sat, deciding to get straight to the point. "So what were you and Mac talking about on the mound tonight?"

"Stuff."

"Me?"

"Let it go, Dani."

"I can't. You told me before that you talked about—"

"Look, I just took exception to his flirting with Tiffany this afternoon, that's all. He took exception to my taking exception."

"Oh." Did that mean Mac was now interested in Tiffany? Was Jason? Were they fighting over her? Was I about to lose my boyfriend? More importantly, was I about to lose Jason as a friend?

"Do you like Tiffany?"

"Of course."

"Does Mac?"

"Ask him."

Too many surly guys in my life tonight. I thought I should just go to bed, worry about everything in the morning, but I was wired from the game, from the altercation.

"Remember that column we brainstormed?" I asked.

"The one about hosting and being hosted?"

"Yeah. I sent the idea to my editor. He doesn't want it for my column. He wants it for a featured article."

"Is that better?"

"Oh, yeah. It's like I'll be a real reporter. Anyway, since you're just sitting there not doing anything, could I go ahead and interview you?"

"I don't know, Dani. I'm kinda wiped out."

"We could start, but stop whenever you tell me. That's the beauty of you living here. We can always pick up later."

He sighed. "Okay."

"Great! I'm going to run up and get my recorder and notebook. I'll be right back."

I stopped by my parents' bedroom, did my usual *knock, knock,* "I'm home!"

"How was the party?" Mom asked groggily.

I chuckled. Some things just never changed. "It was fine."

"Night, sweetie," Mom and Dad said at the same time.

It didn't take me long to grab the things from my bedroom. When I returned to the kitchen, Jason was still there, but the bowl of pickle brine was gone. The room was still a little shadowy.

"Would you be more comfortable somewhere else?" I asked.

"This is fine."

"All righty then." I sat down, turned to an empty page in my notebook, and clicked on the recorder.

"So, this is your first time playing in the collegiate league, right?"

"Right."

"Have you found it hard to adjust to living with . . . strangers?"

"Not really. I have my own room, my own space. I can just hang out there when I need time to myself."

"You've always lived with guys before, right? Brothers, team players—"

"If I don't count my mom."

"For the purposes of this question, she doesn't count."

He grinned. "Then yeah. I've always lived with guys."

"Have you found it different having girls in the house?"

He cleared his throat. "Oh, yeah."

"Would you care to elaborate?"

"Nope."

I looked up from my writing. "If you don't elaborate, it's going to be a very short article."

"Look, I've already gotten into it once tonight—"

"Are you implying I'm hard to live with? Is

that why you won't comment further? Because you think I'll be offended? I won't be."

"No further comment."

I sighed, tempted to toss the recorder at him.

"Okay, then, we'll move on. What's been the most difficult aspect of living with us?"

There was silence, but it was the kind where you can sense someone wants to speak but doesn't. Jason was so incredibly still, as though he was weighing consequences.

"Not kissing you," he finally said, quietly.

My heart did this little stutter. I just stared at him as the recorder continued to run, searching for sound. My hand was shaking when I reached over and turned it off.

"But you did kiss me, and you said it was a mistake."

"Because getting involved with you is a bad idea, on so many levels."

"Care to share one of those levels?"

"I'm living in your house. Your parents are giving me a roof over my head. Your mom brings home extra takeout. I'm here only for the summer. Then I'm back at school." He reached up, removed the ice pack from around his shoulder, and set it on the table. "And Mac? After we went to Dave and Bubba's, he comes out to the mound and tells me he thinks you're hot. And I know you like him, so I was willing to bunt."

"Bunt?"

"Willing to sacrifice my happiness."

"You thought you'd be happy being with me?"

"Are you kidding? You're cute, easy to talk to. You love baseball. You make me smile, make me laugh. And we won't even mention how much I liked kissing you."

Only he *had* mentioned it. And now I was thinking about it when I really shouldn't be.

"Tiffany makes you laugh."

"Oh, yeah, she's funny, says some really silly stuff, but I think she's a lot smarter than she lets on. You, you're honest. You're generous. Talking your parents into providing a home for a player."

Not so honest, not so generous. My reasons

for wanting a player in the house were purely selfish. I wanted someone who would introduce me to the team, introduce the team to me.

"Let's go back to what happened at the ballpark," I said, "because I'm still not getting it."

He sighed. "Look, he tells me he's got a thing for you. I back off. He gets you. And now he's making moves on Tiffany. What's up with that? I know you like him. He's a nine point five and I'm a six—"

"No!" I reached out, covered his hand with mine.

"Dani, I saw your roster that night at Ben and Jerry's, when it fell out of your bag. I unfolded it, shouldn't have, but I did. I saw the hottie scores—"

"No. I mean, yes, I gave you a six, but I did it because I wanted to give you a ten."

He shook his head. "That makes no sense."

"I was trying to convince myself you weren't a ten, because it's a lot harder living with a guy you're attracted to than it is living with one you're not."

"Wait a minute. Let me get this straight. You gave me a six because you liked me, and you thought it would make you stop liking me?"

"I thought it would be weird liking a guy who was living in my house. And I sorta promised Mom I wouldn't do that. Really like the guy who was living here. Only I do."

"But you've been hanging out with Mac."

"Not really. I've been kissing Mac."

I put my elbows on the table, buried my face in my hands. "God, I've created such a mess." I finally lifted my head and looked at him. "I'm not noble. I'm not like Tiffany with her orphans. I talked my parents into sponsoring a player not because guys needed a place to stay. I did it . . . because I wanted a boyfriend."

"You thought I'd be your boyfriend?"

"No, that was too icky to even consider. I mean, you've seen my underwear. I've seen yours."

His mouth twitched.

"I thought you'd introduce me around," I continued. "I'd do things with the team. The players would get to know me, become interested. I just wanted a boyfriend."

It sounded so pathetic, so desperate.

"And now you've got one," he said.

"But I don't know if he's the right one."

He grabbed the ice pack, stood up. "Let me know when you figure it out."

I watched him walk out of the room.

Chapter 20

Jason and Mac. Mac and Jason. I couldn't sleep. Instead, I started working on my feature article, writing it from my perspective.

The hardest part about living with a Rattler?

Finding yourself falling in love with him when you promised your mom you wouldn't.

Who makes a promise like that anyway? Who thinks falling in love is something she has any kind of control over?

The door to my bedroom opened.

"Thought I heard you in here," Tiffany said. "I wanted to get your opinion about something."

I really wasn't in the mood. "I don't want to hear your new-and-improved national anthem."

"Please, it's nowhere near ready to be shared. This is something else." She sat on the edge of the bed, back straight, shoulders square. She was turning into Bree Van De Kamp from *Desperate Housewives*.

"Relax, Tiff. I'm not going to score your posture."

"I am relaxed. Now here's my dilemma. The library and the ASPCA are cosponsoring an event next Saturday: Books 'n' Barks. As Miss Teen Ragland, I will, of course, make an appearance. But I want to do more, because the ASPCA takes in a lot of stray dogs, which are kinda like orphans, and as you're aware, I believe in helping orphans."

She was so serious that as much as I wanted to laugh, I didn't. Instead I reached for my Rattlers autographed baseball and began tossing it between my palms. "Okay."

"I mean, if I do the talk, I should do the walk," she continued. "So I have an idea for something I could do to raise funds, but I'd need some volunteers. A lot of volunteers actually. But I don't know if anyone would want to do it, because it's really kinda yucky."

"Do what?"

"Wash dogs. That's my idea. A dog wash. The event's at the park. They'll have all sorts of vendors selling dog stuff. People will bring their dogs. So I thought I could pay the booth fee and set up a dog wash. People would make a donation to have their dogs washed, and the money would go to the ASPCA."

"I'm impressed, Tiff. That's a great idea."

Her having a great idea was a sobering thought, because if she had in fact gotten brains, too . . . well, I'd been shortchanged.

I'm not sure how she did it, but she sat up even straighter. "Really?"

"Really."

"But who would want to wash dogs? That's my dilemma. Because I sure don't want to do it."

I rolled the baseball around between my hands. "Does it have to be the Tiffany Runyon dog wash?"

"Oh, no, I'm not doing it for my glory. I'm doing it to raise money for orphaned dogs."

I turned to my computer, clicked on my browser, and pulled up the Ragland Rattlers website. I went to their season schedule. Just as I thought. They didn't have a game scheduled for next Saturday.

"How about if you get the Rattlers to volunteer to wash the dogs?"

"Do you think they would?"

"Guys and dogs? Yeah, I think they would."

"Would you talk to them about it?"

"It's your idea. You talk to them."

"No way. I'd end up getting nervous and saying something silly." She tapped her head. "Sometimes I can't believe what I hear myself say. It's, like, engage your brain before you engage your mouth.

"But you're great with those guys. And it's so obvious they adore you. Like at the concert, and the water park. And here at the house? Jason is so relaxed around you. You do things together. At Dad's party, all the guys were relaxed around you. You have things in common, things to talk—"

"Tiffany," I said, cutting her off before she could go on even more. "Guys hang around you all the time. You've had, like, a million dates!"

"With a million guys. Dani, I go out with a guy only once or twice. And it's always soooo awkward. What do we talk about? Nothing. Because how many guys care about the best way to apply mascara or want to discuss the right shade of eye shadow? That's all I know. Beauty tips. So I try to fill the dead air between us and everything always sounds so stupid.

"Don't get me wrong. I *love* being Miss Teen Ragland. But seriously, the whole reason I entered the competition to begin with was to get a boyfriend. Hello?!? It didn't work. And the worst part? Sometimes I am so jealous."

I stared at her, stunned by all she'd said. "Jealous of what?"

"You and the normal life you have."

"It's not normal. I've never had a boyfriend." I was beginning to have doubts that Mac truly counted. Yes, he was a boy, and possibly a friend. But true BF? No longer sure.

"You've got Mac. When we went to get drinks at the concert, all he talked about was how cool you were. And Jason? The way he looks at you sometimes . . . if Mom ever sees that look, the guy will be sleeping in his car."

"How can you say that about Mac? I saw him wrapped around you yesterday—"

"Only because I asked. He is *so* cute. And I was having one of those green-monster moments."

I couldn't believe it. Tiffany was jealous of me? How often had I been jealous of her?

"This look Jason gives me . . . tell me a little more about that."

She shrugged. "He looks like he adores you, like crossing the hallway and knocking on your door crosses his mind sometimes. So, anyway, will you talk to the team? See if they'll volunteer to help out?"

I wanted a little more information about the look, but I knew Tiffany wasn't going to provide any more clarification.

"Sure, I'll talk to them. You could probably get Dad to donate some rubber baseballs the players could autograph. People could make a donation to get a ball to toss to their dogs."

Tiffany flashed one of her dazzling beauty-pageant smiles. "Oh, I like that idea. This could actually be fun."

* * *

"A dog wash?" Bird repeated the next morning.

I'd called her to let her know I needed to talk. She was making her Scoopin' Poopin' runs and had invited me to ride along with her.

I shrugged. "Could be interesting, in a guys-in-wet-T-shirts kind of way."

"Hmm. Hadn't thought of that. Still, it's going to be a lot of work, and you'll be the one who ends up doing it."

"Whatever. It's for a good cause. Orphaned dogs. But that's not really why I called."

"Didn't think it was."

"I was just sorta wondering . . . have you ever noticed the way Jason looks at me?"

She looked in her rearview mirror, looked in her side view mirror.

"Bird?"

"I'm thinking."

"It's not an essay question. It's a yes or no."

"Yes."

"And?"

"Thought you said no essay."

"Come on, Bird, how does he look at me?"

She sighed. "He looks at you like you're something he wants and can't have."

I gazed out the window at the houses passing by. "When have you seen him looking at me like that?"

"When have I *not* seen him looking at you like that?"

"Why didn't you say something?"

She held up a finger. "He lives in your house." Another finger. "I thought you liked Mac."

"I'm so confused, Bird. I wanted a boyfriend."

"And you have one," she said.

"Right. Mac. The problem is, I like Jason so much. And I'm just discovering that maybe he likes me, too. But it would be too weird, with him living in the house."

"Then stick with Mac."

"Is that how you feel about Brandon? That you're 'sticking' with him because he's convenient?"

"No way. I'm totally crazy about him."

And that's what I was discovering. It wasn't enough to have a boyfriend. I wanted someone I was crazy about. As much as I liked Mac, the truth was, he wasn't Jason.

It didn't help matters that the first dog I washed Saturday morning was named Jason. Who gives their dogs people names?

Bird and I had gotten to the park early. We wore oversized T-shirts over our bathing suits and our Ragland Rattlers caps. We'd found spigots, attached water hoses to them, and dragged the hoses to the area designated for our "booth." Even though it was really nothing more than a table and an open area on a knoll where we all had room to move around.

Following the Friday practice, I'd had the guys sign up for the time slot during which they wanted to wash dogs and the time during which they wanted to sit and autograph the rubber balls Dad had donated. Then we had guys sitting at a table, assigning people to a wash team, and taking the donations.

For the first shift, Bird and Brandon were a team, Mac and I were a team, Jason and Ethan were a team. I took control of my team's water hose. Hosing down a dog was a lot less work than lathering him up. Or at least I thought it would be.

Dog-Jason was a black Lab that wanted to play, and he kept trying to leap on me. When Mac and I were finally finished with him, I had wet paw prints all over me.

We sat on the ground, waiting for another dog to be assigned to us.

"That was kinda fun," he said.

"Yeah, it was. And we're helping orphaned dogs."

He glanced around. "Thought you said Tiffany was going to be here."

"I'm sure she'll drop by eventually—as Miss Teen Ragland."

"She is so hot."

"Excuse me, but you're talking about my sister here."

He jerked his head around, his eyes wide. "That was totally uncool, wasn't it?"

"Totally."

"Sorry."

Before I could decide whether or not to accept his apology, someone brought over a Lhasa apso. A sweet little dog that was no trouble to wash. But Mac and I still got sprayed when it did its whole shaking thing to get the water off.

When we were finished, I glanced over at Jason, watching as he washed a little excitable white ball of fur that kept yapping. His efforts made me smile.

"He really likes you, you know," Mac said quietly.

I jerked my head around and stared at him.

He shook his head. "That's what the other night was about. Out on the mound, getting into it going to the dugout. He didn't think I was being a very good boyfriend." Mac started pulling up blades of grass. "The thing is, you and me, I didn't really think of you as my girlfriend. Come the end of the summer, I'll ride into the sunset and not look back." He looked over at me. "So if you're not cool with that . . ."

I swallowed hard. "I'm not sure I am."

"Well, think about it. I'm going to go get us something to drink," Mac said.

Before I could offer any sort of response, he was gone. They'd set up concession booths throughout the park. You could even buy treats for your dogs.

I sorta wondered if he'd even bother to come back. Although he'd used different words than Jason had, he was basically telling me to figure out what I wanted. Who was the right guy?

I glanced back over at Jason. He was still struggling with the little dog. I couldn't help it. I released a bubble of laughter. His head came up, as though he knew I was laughing at him.

"You think this is funny?" he asked.

I shrugged. He sprayed me.

"Hey!" I yelled. I turned on my hose and sent a volley of spray back.

The dog's owner scooped his pet up, said something to Jason I couldn't hear, and walked away.

Jason rose from his crouch, hose in hand. I got to my feet, holding up one hand in defense.

"Okay, look, I didn't mean to laugh—"

He sprayed me again. I shrieked and let him have it, full force. He tried to dodge the spray, tried to hit me with his water, but I darted out of the way, keeping my hose aimed at him. He was getting drenched, absolutely soaked, and I started laughing. It's difficult to run when you're laughing so hard that your sides are hurting.

Jason lunged for me, took me down, somehow rolling so he hit the soaked ground—taking the brunt of the impact—and I landed on top of him. We were both smiling broadly, breathing heavily, totally wet.

Looking into his laughing eyes, I felt as though I'd been slammed with another foul ball.

I was crazy about this guy, absolutely completely crazy about him.

His smile dimmed. His gaze wandered to my mouth. I could see clearly how much he wanted to kiss me. And I knew he wouldn't.

So I kissed him.

And he kissed me back.

"Excuse me, but we're supposed to be raising money for orphaned dogs."

I looked up to find Tiffany standing there in jeans; her Miss Teen Ragland sash draped across her gold, sparkly tank top; and her tiara reflecting the sunlight enough to give me a headache.

I don't know what possessed me. But I sprayed her.

She released a shrill screech, backed up, and glared at me, with water dripping down her face. "I can't believe you did that!"

"You need to relax," I said as I scrambled off Jason.

"Excuse me?"

"When was the last time you had fun?"

"I'm here as—"

"I know. Miss Teen Ragland. But this is your setup, your idea."

She jerked back as I reached out and grabbed her hand.

"You're gonna wash some dogs," I said.

"No way!"

"Yes way!"

I pulled her toward where I'd left the shampoo. "Hey!" I yelled to no one in particular. "I need a dog and a couple of guys to help."

Mac stepped in front of me. "I'll help her."

When had he returned?

"Mac—" I could tell he'd seen me with Jason. I don't know what I was going to say. Apologize? Tell him I had thought about things?

"We make a lousy team, anyway," he said.

I wasn't sure I'd go so far as to declare us

lousy, but he was giving me an easy out. Gratefully, I took it.

Grabbing the hose, he looked at Tiffany. "I'll do the work, you spray the water."

I quickly pressed a finger against Tiffany's mouth. "Don't say anything for a while, not until you're comfortable."

She nodded.

"Just be Tiffany," I said quietly. "And we'll charge double to anyone who wants Miss Teen Ragland to wash their dog."

She nodded again, looking over to where Ethan and Mac were soaping up a collie.

"They're just guys, Tiff."

She nodded one more time before walking over to become part of a team. I heard her say, "So what kind of dog is this?"

As far as questions went, it wasn't a bad one.

I couldn't hear Mac's response, but while Ethan continued to scrub the dog, Mac stood up, put his hand over Tiffany's, and helped her guide the direction of the spray. She looked up at him and smiled. Not a Miss Teen Ragland smile. But a Tiffany smile.

And Mac looked absolutely dazzled.

"So what now?" Jason asked.

"I guess I need to find someone to help me wash."

"I'm available."

I faced him. "I have a feeling I'm available, too."

And I knew neither of us was talking about washing dogs.

"We don't have a game tomorrow, and the coaches have rented a bus. They're taking us to Ameriquest Field to watch the Rangers play, like a field trip. Anyway, we can invite someone to go with us. Want to come?"

Was he serious? Did he really think I'd say no to the opportunity to watch the Texas Rangers?

But more importantly, it was an invitation for an official date. Not an appreciation outing. I mean, usually you have the date before you have the kiss, but then I wasn't a real stickler when it came to traditions. I could go with the flow.

"I'd love to go."

"Great."

"Yeah," I said, smiling. "Great."

Chapter 21

"Omigod! I need help!"

I'd just pulled my Ragland Rattlers T-shirt on above my denim shorts when Tiffany burst into the room in a full-scale panic the next morning.

My heart started to thunder. "What's wrong?"

"I don't know what to wear."

I stared at her as my heart resumed its normal beat.

"Excuse me?"

"Mac invited me to go to this ball game with him today . . . and it's, like, what do I wear?"

I grinned and pointed to my hat rack. "Pick a cap, any cap."

"You're not serious?"

"Tiff, it's a ball game in an open stadium. And we're riding a bus to get there. You want cool and comfortable."

She held up her hand and closed her eyes like the thought frightened her. "Just *tell* me exactly what to wear."

She did the whole makeup thing, of course. I fixed her hair. Pulled it back into a ponytail.

"One elastic fits all," I said, grinning at her in the mirror.

She was wearing a pair of designer jeans and one of my older Ragland Rattler T-shirts. I settled a cap on her head, pulled her strands of hair through the opening in the back.

"There, you're all ready to go," I said.

She peered in the mirror, and I could see the doubts crossing her face. "I guess it doesn't look too bad."

"You look great."

She swiveled around. "Are you okay with me going with Mac?"

"I'm fine with it. He and I . . . we never really connected."

"He's so funny."

"He is?"

She nodded. "He says I make him feel like an Internet search engine with all my questions, but he's okay with it."

"He thinks you're hot."

"Really?"

How could she doubt that any guy would find her hot?

"Yeah, he mentioned it yesterday."

"I just don't want to embarrass him at the game."

"You won't."

"And don't take offense, but we're not going to hang out near you, because that would be too weird, since you were dating him."

"Not a problem."

"You and Jason . . . it's a date, isn't it?"

"Um . . . yeah."

"Probably shouldn't tell Mom and Dad."

"Probably not. At least not yet. I mean, it might not work out."

"Puh-lease! Have a little faith in yourself."

Miss Teen Ragland had just delivered encouragement.

* * *

Jason and I were holding hands in the parking lot of the Ragland ballpark, waiting for the bus to arrive. He was wearing jeans and a Ragland Rattlers baseball jersey.

As a matter of fact, all the guys were wearing the same thing. I figured they had to go as representatives of the team.

"Tiffany and Mac?" Bird whispered, when she and Brandon joined us.

Tiffany and Mac were standing a short distance away, talking. Actually talking. Imagine that.

I shrugged. "What can I say?"

Then we heard the bus rattling up the street. It was an old school bus.

"Ah, man," Jason said. "For this event, I thought they'd use something other than our usual transport to the games. I thought it would be . . . you know . . . one of those air-conditioned fancy buses."

"We're not in the majors yet," Brandon said.

"I'm really sorry," Jason said.

"Hey, no big deal."

"Let's at least get on first, so we can sit in

the back," Bird suggested.

Everyone seemed to have the same idea. By the time Jason and I got on, the only seat I saw was the one right behind the bus driver. And two of the coaches were sitting across the aisle. I so didn't want to sit there. Then I heard someone calling my name—near the back of the bus.

And there was Bird, jumping up and down, waving her arm. Not quite at the back, but close enough. She was on one seat and Brandon was in the seat behind her. I don't know how she managed to get on the bus so far ahead of us, but I wasn't going to complain.

Jason and I made our way back there, and Bird hopped out of the seat and sat beside Brandon. I slid in so I was beside the window. The window was down. I thought about putting it back up, but it was almost a hundred degrees outside. And the bus wasn't air-conditioned. I was sorta wishing I'd worn skimpier clothes.

"All right!" one of the coaches yelled. "I'm going to call out the roster and make sure everyone is here."

After Jason answered to his name being

called, he looked at me and grinned. "So have you ever watched the Rangers play in person?"

"Oh, yeah."

The coach finished calling the roster. Everyone was there, so we took off. With the wind blowing through the windows, we all had to remove our caps. My hair was whipping around my face. I heard a screech from the front of the bus. Tiffany, learning to deal with flying hair.

There was too much wind noise to talk. Bird tried to start a conversation, but it just didn't work when we had to yell in each other's ears. The ride was really bumpy. Not exactly the perfect atmosphere for an official first date.

Of course, we weren't the only busload of people to arrive at the ballpark. We had quite a little hike across the parking lot, but I didn't mind because Jason was holding my hand again.

"First stop, concession stand," Brandon said. "I'm starving."

"I don't know if I can ever eat concession-stand food again," Bird said. "Now that I know how hard they work."

"But these people are paid, Bird," I reminded her.

"Oh, that's different then, isn't it?"

"Most definitely."

Jason handed me my ticket. "If the bus ride is any indication of what we can expect, I suspect the seats aren't anything to write home about."

"Do you write home?" I asked.

"I e-mail my mom and brothers," he said. "Now and then."

"Will they ever come watch you play?"

"Probably not. They come to the university games, but they're busy with their own lives, and I don't think they're that interested in the collegiate league."

I couldn't imagine that.

"I love the collegiate league," Bird said, snuggling up against Brandon.

We went through the gate and headed for the concession stand. The guys got in line. We obviously weren't the only ones with food on our minds.

Bird and I headed for the ladies' room. Tiffany was there, brushing out her tangles.

"So what do you think so far, Tiff?" I asked as I started combing my hair.

"I'm thinking next year we need to have some sort of fund-raiser. These guys deserve better than old school buses."

"If anyone can make it happen, it's Miss Teen Ragland."

"Next year, I'll just be Tiffany."

She put on her cap, and I tugged on the brim. "I think Tiffany can make it happen, too."

"Especially since you and Bird will be on my committee."

She walked out before we could respond.

"Did she just volunteer us?" Bird asked.

"Yep." I dropped my comb into my tote. I put my cap and sunglasses back on. Next year's fund-raising committee was the last thing I wanted to think about. For the next couple of hours, I planned to focus on this year's team, this year's pitcher.

Tonight's date.

While the odds seemed against it, we somehow ended up with our seats together: Brandon, Bird, me, and Jason, in that order. We were surrounded by other team players. Tiffany and Mac were several rows above us, which assured Tiffany and I remained comfortable with our dates.

"I can't believe it," Bird said. "How did you guys manage to get our tickets together?"

"We knew you'd want to sit together," Brandon said, leaning over and kissing her. "So we made it happen."

I had a feeling there was going to be a lot of kissing going on between those two.

"Hope the seats are okay with you," Jason said.

"They're great." I squeezed his hand. "Really great."

Our drink was in the cup holder between us. We were sharing a drink, but had our own hot dogs. Nothing's better than a ballpark frank.

We finished eating just as they asked us to stand for the national anthem. After the song ended—with no additional flourishes—they welcomed the Ragland Rattlers to the game, flashing our team name on one of the big screens. We all started yelling, waving our hats.

"I wish we'd brought our rattles!" I yelled over the crowd. If we'd known that we'd be recognized, Bird and I would have for sure.

We took our seats and the game began. It got really quiet in our section, and I realized these guys weren't really here for the enjoyment of the game. They were here to pick up tips. Jason was leaning forward, his elbows on his thighs, watching the windup, watching the pitch, following the ball.

I leaned forward, too. "Do you find it hard to be loyal to a team that you're only a temporary member of?"

He glanced over at me. "What brought on that question?"

"Well, you're here as a member of the Ragland Rattlers, but I'd think deep down, you see yourself as a member of your college team. I mean, if a reporter asked what team you play for, wouldn't you say the University of Texas?"

He nodded slowly. "Yeah, I would, but that doesn't mean I don't feel any loyalty to Ragland. I mean, I'll play my best until the end of the season."

"I know you will. But it must feel strange."

"A little, yeah. I mean, there are guys on the team who I'll be pitching against next season. I'll be trying to strike them out; they'll be trying to get a hit off me. It won't be anything personal. It's all about the sport."

Austin was a four-hour drive from Ragland. "Maybe I'll come watch you play next season," I said.

"That'd be great."

And I knew I was getting way ahead of myself, but when he was looking at me like that, looking at me instead of the players on the field, I thought. *Yeah, I'll go to Austin and watch you play.*

Jason turned his attention back to the game.

"These guys are watching the game like it's a homework assignment," Bird said after a while, leaning forward so she could talk to me in a low voice.

"It's their jobs, I guess. It's probably hard to take pleasure in something that is so important to you. When I'm a reporter, I'll probably stop actually watching the news that's being covered and focus instead on *how* it's being covered. I'll listen to voice inflections and observe various stances. That sort of thing."

The cotton candy vendor walked down the aisle. Bird and I each bought a bag—blue for her, pink for me. It was a real treat, because we didn't sell cotton candy at the Ragland field. I pulled off a wisp of sugar and felt it melt as soon as my tongue touched it.

I looked over at Jason. "Want some?"

He grinned. "Sure."

I pulled some off, held it out to him. He opened his mouth slightly, a challenge in his eyes. I don't know why I'd thought he'd take it from me.

Finally, he said, "I don't want to get my fingers sticky."

Oh, right. I got really warm, but I pushed the cotton candy into his mouth—and couldn't help thinking about a bride shoving the cake into the groom's mouth.

Jason's lips barely touched my fingers as his mouth closed, and I pulled back, but I got that much hotter, had felt his breath skim across my knuckles. It was so intimate, so personal, like something you'd do with someone you had a serious crush on. Much more intimate than spooning him ice cream. With ice cream, there was the distance of the spoon, not to mention that it was cold.

"I haven't had cotton candy in forever," he said. "I'd forgotten how . . . sugary it is."

"It's pure sugar."

"I wonder who invented it."

"I think it was a dentist."

He laughed, a laugh that revealed his perfect smile, his perfect teeth. "I'll bet you're right."

There was the crack of the bat, and our attention was once more on the game.

Between the fourth and fifth innings, they had the Kiss Cam going around. A heart was displayed on a big screen in the stadium and a camera would zoom in on a couple. The couple would then kiss. There was an older couple with white hair—had to be married. Then they moved on to a couple of kids, who just laughed and waved.

Then there was Jason and me. On the big screen. A big red heart around us. I felt my face turn as red as that heart. I heard Bird squeal and felt her punch my arm, thought I heard Tiffany shriek behind me.

"Kiss him!" Bird ordered.

The camera stayed on us. I knew it would until we kissed. I turned my head to look at Jason, but he was already there, kissing me, while the spectators screamed and applauded, especially the Ragland Rattlers.

I guess it was official—we were on a date.

The Kiss Cam seemed to trigger the real start of our date . . . or maybe it just served as an ice breaker where kissing was concerned. Because after the entire stadium had seen us kiss, Jason wasn't quite so shy about kissing me anymore. Not long, slow kisses, not the kind of kisses that you didn't want broadcast on national TV, but kisses just the same.

Whenever the pitcher struck out someone . . . kiss.

When the Rangers got a hit . . . kiss.

When they got a run . . . . longer kiss.

He held my hand, smiled at me, and just seemed really glad that I was there. I was glad I was there, too.

During the seventh inning stretch, we stood up and sang "Take Me Out to the Ball Game." Jason and I swayed together. I couldn't have been happier.

The Rangers won.

"See how it makes a difference when rituals are honored?" Jason said, his arm around my waist keeping me anchored against his side.

"I'm too happy to argue," I said.

We stopped off in the gift shop, and he bought me a Texas Rangers cap.

"Maybe you can start decorating a wall with caps from the games *we* go to," he said.

I grinned broadly, because I knew what he was really saying: Tonight was just the beginning for us.

It had grown dark by the time the game ended. The air had cooled off a fraction. Everything seemed so much quieter as we walked to the bus.

"Saw you on the Kiss Cam," Tiffany said when we got behind her and Mac, waiting to get on the bus. They were holding hands. She looked happy.

Mac and Jason did that whole nodding at each other thing.

Somehow Jason and I ended up on the very last seat. Maybe everyone else was just too tired to walk that far.

Jason put his arm around me and drew me up against his side. Once the coach called the roster and everyone was accounted for, we headed home. It was really dark on the bus. It didn't seem as windy. Maybe because Jason was holding me close.

Then he kissed me. A really long, slow, deep kiss. A kiss that made me see fireworks.

When he pulled back, I could see him grinning, even in the darkness. "I love the flavor of chocolate chip cookie dough ice cream."

"You know where you can always get a taste," I said.

He kissed me again.

Chapter 22

We kissed pretty much the entire bus ride home. Jason was a fantastic kisser.

When the bus finally arrived at the Ragland ballpark, I said good-bye to Bird, then Jason took my hand and led me to his car. I didn't see Mac and Tiffany, but since they'd been sitting at the front of the bus, I assumed they were already on their way home. I figured Mac was feeling a little strange spending time with my sister, after spending time with me.

But I was totally okay with it. It wasn't like we'd ever really connected. And from the beginning, I'd felt like he'd only become interested after he saw me as a Tiffany clone. So now he had the real thing.

Jason held my hand as we drove home.

When we arrived, Mac's car was in the drive, so Jason kept going. He made a couple of circuits around the block, until Mac's car was no longer there.

Jason pulled into the driveway, turned off the car, and kissed me.

Then it got kinda weird. It was like: Where should our last kiss be?

In the car? At the door? Inside the foyer? Outside my bedroom?

I just didn't know. I'd avoided giving any real thought to how I would go about having a boyfriend living in my house. I mean, I'd never planned for the guy I fell for to be living in my house, across the hallway. What if my parents figured it out?

We would have to be so careful.

Jason drew back from the kiss and pressed his forehead to mine.

"You know I could kiss you all night," he said.

"Me, too."

I was such a romantic, but I was also nervous, because I knew no way we were going to be kissing in my parents' house all night.

"But I'm feeling kinda weird about it," he said.

"That whole liking-the-daughter-of-the-people-who-are-giving-you-a-roof-over-your-head thing?"

"Yeah."

"I know. If my parents caught us . . ."

"Yeah."

"Maybe we need house rules."

He pulled back. "Like what?"

"No kissing inside the house."

"Ever?"

"Well, at least not when Mom and Dad are home. Dad jokes about putting potential boyfriends through an interview process, but he may be serious. It's hard to tell sometimes with him."

"It felt like he was interviewing me that first night."

"Not to be my boyfriend."

He sighed. "Okay. I see your point."

"So how are we going to handle this?"

"This is going to sound strange, but what if we pretend, for the next ten minutes, that I don't live here. I'll walk you to the door. You go inside, then I'll get back in my car and drive around the block."

I giggled. "That seems a little drastic."

"Yeah, but if we don't do it like this I'm going to be kissing you all the way to your room. We sorta need to break the cycle."

"Okay."

He kissed me again. Slow. So slow. His fingers in my hair. His thumb drawing a circle on my cheek.

He drew back. "Okay."

He opened the car door and climbed out. I opened the door on my side, and by the time I got out, he was standing there. He took my hand, gave me a quick kiss, and led me to the front porch where my parents had left the light on.

"I had a really nice time," I said with a very serious face.

He chuckled lightly. "Yeah, me, too. Maybe we could go out again sometime."

I almost burst out laughing. "I'd like that."

"Good night, Dani," he said quietly.

Then he took me in his arms and gave me a good-night kiss to remember.

When he stepped back, I was really sorry to see him go, but I knew we couldn't stay out there forever.

"Good night," I said. I turned to the door, slipped my key into the lock, then turned back around. "You'll call me, right?"

He laughed, ducked his head slightly, and grinned at me. "Yeah, I'll call you."

"If you don't, I'll short-sheet your bed."

With that, I slipped inside, closed the door, and pressed my ear against it, wondering if he was really going to get in his car and drive around the block.

I heard a car door slam, heard him start the engine . . .

I was giddy, so very happy. It seemed silly for him to drive around the block, but on the other hand, it seemed like the perfect way to actually signal the end of our date. I mean, we weren't married, but we were living in the same house.

Mom had left a light on in the kitchen. And knowing Mom, she was awake, too. I walked to my parents' bedroom door and knocked on it.

"I'm home."

"How was the game?" Mom asked.

"It was fun."

"Night, hon."

"Night."

I went upstairs, thought about going to bed. That would have been the smart thing to do. Instead I went into the game room and turned on the TV.

And waited.

But when the door clicked open, it wasn't Jason, it was Tiffany.

She sat beside me. "Hey."

"So how'd you like the game?" I asked.

"It was okay. I liked being with Mac a whole lot, so I guess I have to start liking baseball."

"You'll feel different about it when you're watching him play."

"What are you going to do about Jason?" she asked.

"What do you mean?"

"You promised Mom."

"Yeah, I know."

"So?"

I shook my head. "I don't know yet, Tiff."

"I just want you to know that I won't say anything, but it seems to me that it's something that will be really hard to keep a secret."

Yeah, it would be. I'd always been honest with my parents.

"I'll figure something out."

"Well, I'm going to bed." She got up. "Unless, you know, you need me to stay to make sure—"

"I don't need you to stay."

"Okay then. Night."

It was a long while later before I heard footsteps on the stairs. Jason looked into the game room, grinned, and opened the door. "I was hoping I'd find you here."

"What took you so long?"

He held up the DVD for *The Rookie* and a bag from Ben & Jerry's.

Grinning, I patted the love seat. We could be together in the house without getting into trouble.

At least, we could try.

Chapter 23

The next morning, I was lying in bed, staring at the ceiling, trying to figure out exactly how to handle this relationship with Jason, because I thought it was safe to say that we did indeed have a relationship.

And we were living in the same house, and that was kinda strange. If I saw him in the hallway, did I just say hi? Did I kiss him good morning? Should I fix him some breakfast?

I could pour cereal into a bowl. I could slice bananas.

I heard a shower go on, a distant shower, not in the bathroom next to my room, but in the one across the hall, which meant it was Jason.

He'd taken at least one shower, usually two a day in that bathroom. So why was I suddenly freaked out by the thought of him in the shower? Naked?

Oh, gosh, this was insane. What if he opened the door to my bedroom? What if he came inside? What if he wanted to give me a good-morning kiss?

Okay, that was so not going to happen. Hadn't we said no kissing in the house?

Not that the rule had stopped us from kissing in the game room last night after we'd finished our ice cream.

"I'm still craving the flavor of chocolate chip cookie dough," he'd said.

So of course, I'd let him sample.

But it had been . . . stressful.

Because every time the house creaked, we were looking at the French doors expecting to see Dad standing there with a baseball bat in hand.

So I was pretty sure Jason wasn't going to come into my room. Even if my parents had already left for work.

He was going to finish his shower, go downstairs for breakfast, then go to work, then to practice.

I was trying to decide whether or not to call Bird and invite her to go to lunch with me at Ruby Tuesday. If we did that, then I'd see Jason pretty much all day. And if Bird wasn't available, maybe Tiffany would be interested.

Was I really considering hanging out with Tiffany? How weird was that?

Besides, I was certain she had something to deliver somewhere.

I was pathetic. I wanted to be with Jason all day, and I couldn't, because he had commitments. But I could watch him, at least.

Would that make me a stalker?

I heard his shower go off. Okay. I had to do something. I had to decide. Did I want to be out in the hallway when he came out of his bedroom? I hadn't even brushed my teeth yet. No way was I going to say good morning if I hadn't brushed my teeth.

I heard another shower start up. Tiffany! She'd beat me to the shower.

What was it about wanting what you couldn't have?

I got out of bed, knocked on the bathroom door, and walked in.

"Hello?!? I'm in the shower," she said.

"I'm just going to brush my teeth. Besides, you've never been modest before."

I grabbed my toothbrush. "Uh, say, did you want to go to Ruby Tuesday for lunch?"

Had I really asked?

"Can't. I have to go practice the national anthem. July Fourth is only a couple of days away."

"Oh, right. How's that new-and-improved version going, by the way?"

"It's going great."

Terrific. I wasn't really thrilled to hear that, but I knew Tiffany's mind was set.

I brushed my teeth in record time, pulled my hair back, then changed into my scruffy hang-around-the-house shorts and a tank. I went into the hallway. The door to Jason's room was open, so I hurried past and went down the stairs.

I found him in the kitchen, at the table in the bay window, already eating his cereal.

"I was going to fix you breakfast," I said.

He grinned. "I wouldn't want you to put yourself out."

"No one can pour cereal like I can. That's true."

I crossed the kitchen. He scooted his chair back, and I sat on his lap and put my arms on his shoulders.

"Good morning," I said, right before I kissed him.

Oh, yes, this was definitely the way to start the day.

"We're in the house," he said when we stopped kissing. "Thought we had a rule about not kissing in the house."

"Yeah, we also had a house rule—no falling for the player living with us. You see how good I am at following rules."

He grinned. "Lucky for me. Why don't you come to Ruby Tuesday for lunch?"

"Okay."

"Then practice."

"Definitely."

"Maybe we could do something afterward."

"Absolutely."

He kissed me again. He tasted like bran flakes and raisins and bananas.

Me, I tasted like chocolate chip cookie dough.

It was an odd combination but it somehow worked.

Chapter 24

"Telling the guy I've come to think of as a son that he's got to move out."

Dad had agreed to be interviewed for my article.

And *that* was his response to my question about the most difficult part of having a Ragland Rattler living in the house.

I sat at the table in the kitchen, stunned, staring at him. It was only Day One following our trek to the Rangers' game. We hadn't even *seen* Mom and Dad since we got home last night, at least not until fifteen minutes ago when we'd returned from practice. And we'd been so careful not to look at each other, not to touch, not to even grin at each other.

No way could they have figured out what

was going on between Jason and me!

Right now he was upstairs taking a shower, since he was all grimy following practice. Tiffany had taken Mac to Lettuce Eat, a salad bar extravaganza. I couldn't see *that* working out, but if it did, I figured Mac's feelings for her were true. Mom was setting Cowboy Bob's rotisserie chicken, hash brown casserole, and sweet corn casserole on the counter, so we could serve ourselves buffet style.

"Why . . . why do you think you need to do that?" I asked.

Dad touched his glasses. "These work you know."

"Only for close up."

Shaking his head, he gave me an indulgent grin. "Dani, your mom and I were young once. We see the way you and Jason look at each other."

I glanced over at Mom. She was leaning against the counter, her arms crossed.

"I know I promised—" I began.

"Sweetie, no girl is going to keep that kind of promise when she starts falling for a guy. But you could have said something."

"Like what?"

"Like . . . 'we have problem.'"

"In all honesty, we didn't realize we had a problem until last night," Jason said from the doorway.

My heart lurched at the sight of him holding his duffle bag.

"You don't have to move out," I said coming to my feet. I turned to my dad. "Tell him, tell him he doesn't have to move out."

"Yeah, I do, Dani." Jason looked at my parents. "I talked with Coach after practice. I'm going to bunk at his place." He grinned, actually grinned, while I was rushing into full-scale panic at the thought of him leaving. "Coach says he always keeps a bedroom available for just such an emergency."

"Well, son," Dad said, "I'm sure glad you took the initiative on that, because I wasn't looking forward to talking to you about it."

I couldn't believe it. Jason was moving out. We'd only really just discovered each other.

Jason pulled a folded piece of paper out of his jeans pocket. "Actually, I signed a contract stating I'd move out if I kissed either of your daughters more than twice."

"The League makes you sign a contract?" I asked, dumbfounded.

"Uh, no, your mom did, that first night."

"Mom!" I couldn't believe she did that.

"Like your dad said, I was young once."

"Why didn't you tell me you were going to move out?" I asked Jason.

"Because I thought you might try to talk me out of it."

I scowled at him. I would have.

Mom smiled. "Why don't you stay for dinner?"

"I'm going to miss all the takeout," Jason said later, after dinner, when I walked him out to his car. "Coach said his wife cooks their meals every night."

"That's really why you're leaving, isn't it?" I asked. "For real home-cooked meals?"

He put his hands on my waist, drew me near. "If you knew how hard I found it to stay on my side of the hall last night after we finished watching the movie . . ." He shook his head. "Your parents absolutely wouldn't approve of the direction that my thoughts are going. With or without your mom's contract, I'd move out."

"I can't believe she did that."

He grinned. "Yeah, it was that first night, after she came out of your room."

"Weren't you offended?"

"How could I be? I started falling for you as soon as you bumped into me. I knew I could be a goner so easily."

"Really?"

"Oh, yeah. And when I pictured you in shoulder pads and a helmet—"

I shoved his shoulder. "You did not!"

"Oh, yeah, I did. And I thought, of all the girls in this town, she is the *one* that I absolutely can't find fascinating."

"Is that the reason you sounded like you really didn't want to take me home after that first night of pizza?"

"Yep. I wanted to limit contact. I was trying so hard not to fall for you."

"Well, that's why I knocked you over," I said. He laughed.

"Will you still come play ball with Dad?"

"Sure. But you have to play, too."

I smiled. "Okay."

It was so, so hard—a dozen kisses later—watching him leave. But at least I knew he'd be back. There was a free concert tomorrow night. Maybe we'd go.

After Jason left, I went into the backyard. Dad was sitting on the deck, doing some sketching. Another project for someone's backyard.

"Hey, Dad, want to play a little pitch?"

He did his Bruce Willis grin. "You bet. You're still my favorite ball-tosser."

Chapter 25

The Fourth of July game against the Denton Outlaws was a sellout. I was practically sitting in Bird's lap behind home plate.

I hadn't seen Jason before the game. His living in another house had definite drawbacks. But it also had its perks.

Only a couple of days had passed since he'd moved out, but when we were together there was an intensity to it, because we knew our time was short. We made the most of every minute. Kissing, laughing, talking about nothing and everything.

Big surprise. Mom had instituted a curfew. Like there was something we'd do after midnight that we wouldn't do before. But neither of us was bothered by her restrictions. Between

Jason working, practicing, and playing, we weren't going to stay out that late anyway. Still, I did miss watching movies and sharing ice cream with him late into the night.

But that morning, on his way to work, he'd dropped off a box—and a kiss. A couple of kisses, actually.

Have I mentioned that he's a terrific kisser? Long, slow kisses, exactly the way that I knew I'd like them.

After he left I opened the box. Inside I found a note:

For tonight's game.
—J

And a jersey. RATTLERS was written across the front. On the left side and on the back was the number eleven. Jason's number.

I was wearing it now with jeans, sneakers, and my Ragland Rattlers baseball cap. As soon as the game ended, they were going to shoot off fireworks. Bird and I planned to join the team on the field when that happened. Or more accurately, join our boyfriends.

Mom didn't usually come to the ball games, but she was there tonight, sitting on the top row with Dad, video camera at the ready.

Because, of course, Tiffany was walking onto the field. She was wearing red leather boots, a blue jean skirt, and a shirt that looked a lot like the Texas flag with one huge white stripe, one red stripe, and a patch of blue with a white star on it. A red bandanna graced her throat. The tiara sitting on her hair reflected the setting sun.

"She does realize this game isn't televised, doesn't she?" Bird asked.

"When you are Miss Teen Ragland, you are always on stage," I said, repeating something Tiffany had told me.

She was still spending time with Mac. It wasn't awkward seeing them together. Now that I was with Jason, I'd come to realize that Mac had never really been my boyfriend. He'd simply been the guy who . . . well, just the *guy*, really. The guy I stood or sat next to. The guy I'd sometimes kissed.

He hadn't been the guy who made my heart pound or my smile broaden or my happiness increase. He hadn't been the one with whom I wanted to share moments. He wasn't the one for whom I'd designated a section of my bedroom wall for marking memories.

Every night before I went to bed, I touched the Rangers cap hanging on the wall and wondered what other caps might join it. Jason had been talking about us driving to Oklahoma City to watch a Redhawks game. After that, who knew?

"If you'll all stand for the national anthem," the announcer boomed over the sound system.

Along with everyone else, I got to my feet. I looked at the players lined up along the baseline, hats over their hearts. I spotted Jason, and wondered if I'd ever known such contentment at a ball game, if I'd ever really felt that I was so much a part of a game that I wasn't actually playing in.

"Singing the national anthem tonight, we are honored to have with us Miss Teen Ragland, Tiffany Runyon," the announcer continued.

Tiffany raised her hand and waved, like she was sitting on a float, while the crowd clapped and cheered. I put my fingers in my mouth and whistled.

When the crowd quieted, Tiffany began to sing without any music accompanying her.

All I can say is that she belted out that song like she was standing on the deck of a ship watching the rockets' red glare. She didn't hold the notes longer than they should have been held or add any extra notes to the song. She sang it the way it was supposed to be sung.

I couldn't have been more proud of her.

"Wow, that was a surprise," Bird said, after the cheers died down and we took our seats again. "She's really good."

"Yeah," I said. "She really is."

We settled in to watch the game. Brandon was on first base. Jason was on the mound. Bird and I shook our rattles.

"What are you going to do when summer is over, Bird?"

"Start my senior year."

I knocked my rattle on her knee. "I mean about Brandon."

She shrugged. "Your cool idea wasn't so cool after all. I don't know what we're going to do. He goes to Texas Tech, out in West Texas. I'll never see him. What about you and Jason?"

"Austin isn't too far away. We might be able to make it work."

"I just wanted a summer boyfriend."

"Me, too. Only now I want a forever boyfriend."

"Yeah."

She said it like it was the worst thing in the world to want.

"You're going to come to the party afterward, right?" she asked.

"You bet. Wouldn't miss it."

It was another opportunity to be with Jason. I usually ate lunch at Ruby Tuesday. And of course, I always came to watch his practices.

We'd gone to another concert. It had been a violinist. We'd been the only non-silver-haired people there. When you're poor, you can't be choosy about your entertainment, but that doesn't mean you can't have the best time ever.

Jason struck out the first, second, and third batters.

"Do *not* go talk to him," Bird said.

"No problem."

"Don't even look at him," she said.

"Now, that I can't do. He's so cute."

"Hey, guys," Tiffany said, calling out to us from the steps.

"Hey, Tiff. Loved what you did with the national anthem," I said.

"Didn't do anything with it."

"I know. That's the reason I loved it."

"Is there room for me to sit with y'all?"

Not really, but she was, after all, Miss Teen Ragland. And my sister.

"Sure," I said. "We'll make room."

I scrunched up next to Bird.

"It's a good thing I like you," she whispered.

Tiffany made her way down the row and sat beside me.

"So who's up to bat?" she asked.

"Alan."

She knew the players now because she'd started coming to the practices to watch Mac. She was going to be so thrilled when I told her that I'd signed her up to work concessions with Bird and me next week. Hey, you do the talk, you do the walk.

"Oh, and Mac's in the batter's box," she

said, her voice laced with excitement.

This was the first time she'd actually seen him play, because the Rattlers hadn't had any games since we went to the Rangers game.

I leaned toward her. "Any minute now he's going to—"

Look into the stands and grin, touch his helmet. Tiffany waved at him.

"Isn't he to die for?" she asked.

"Absolutely." Still a nine point five. While my guy . . . well, I'd decided to be honest and change his hottie score to ten point five. The only one on the roster.

Alan got to first base, and Mac stepped up to the plate.

Tiffany squeezed my hand. "Oh, I hope he does good."

"He will."

Mac bunted. Tiffany stood, started clapping, and yelling for him to run! Run! Run!

The ball rolled toward the pitcher, who quickly picked it up and slung it to first base.

Stunned, Tiffany sat down as Mac trotted across the field toward the dugout. She leaned toward me. "I thought he'd hit the ball harder."

"That's called a bunt. He did it on purpose, so the guy on first could get to second. It's called making a sacrifice."

"But if he'd hit a home run, the guy could have gotten home."

"Home runs are rare, Tiff."

"Still, it seems like you should always try."

"He has to do what the coaches tell him. They told him to bunt."

"Well, I don't think much of that strategy."

I felt like I'd fallen into an alternate universe. Who would have thought I'd ever be talking baseball with Tiffany? The next thing I knew, she'd be joining Dad and me for our after-dinner pitch sessions.

Jason was the next batter. He did his whole Velcro routine. Then he stepped up to the plate.

The first ball went past.

"Strike!"

I groaned. "Come on, Jason."

He swung at the second.

I didn't realize I was squeezing Tiffany's and Bird's hands until Bird said, "You know, bones break under pressure."

"Oh, sorry." I tried holding my own hands, but it wasn't as comforting.

The next ball was actually a ball. As a matter of fact, so were the two that followed, which gave Jason a full count. I hated full counts. I hated the pressure he was under. I just wanted him to have a good game.

But no matter how he batted or pitched, I'd still love everything about him. Because it wasn't the ballplayer I'd fallen for. It was the actual guy. Jason. Even if he didn't play ball, I'd be crazy about him.

For the briefest of seconds, it was like he looked back into the stands, like maybe he spotted me, shaking my rattle, giving him all the encouragement I could. I could have sworn I saw a corner of his mouth curl up. Then he did the whole Velcro batting glove thing and stepped up to the plate.

The pitch came.

He swung.

Crack!

He hit it! He hit it! I jumped up and started shouting.

I had a second to see the stunned look on

his face, like maybe he'd never hit the ball before, but that couldn't be . . .

And then I realized what it was. As he started running, he turned his head, his gaze following the ball . . .

The ball that went out of the ballpark!

Right over the Backyard Mania billboard!

Home run!

My boyfriend had hit a home run!

I jumped around, pointing at the number on my jersey, hugging Bird, hugging Tiffany, watching Jason slapping his coach's hand as he rounded third. I watched him cross home plate, wearing the biggest grin on his face.

"You know what this means, don't you?" Bird said.

"That we're ahead two to nothing?"

"It means he'll insist you sit in this exact spot for every game. He'll think this is the good luck spot."

"No way."

"Either that, or he'll ask you not to wash your underwear."

"Ew! That's so not happening. Maybe I can

convince him it was wearing the jersey."

Yeah, I thought. *That's the ticket.*

The rest of the game was actually a let-down. No more home runs. No more runs, period. Very few hits actually. The Rattlers ended up winning two to zero.

Awesome!

The players were going onto the field. The announcer was explaining that they'd welcome host families joining the players, but others should stay in the stands while they readied the fireworks.

"Come on," I said, grabbing Tiffany's and Bird's hands.

I think most people were ignoring the announcer, because a lot of them were scrambling onto the field. And by the time we got there, I was sorta wishing I'd stayed in the stands.

I lost track of Bird and Tiffany, but I figured they'd gone off to hook up with Brandon and Mac.

"Good game," someone said, patting my shoulder.

"Thanks," I said, laughing.

Then I felt arms come around me and pull me close.

"Hey," Jason said, kissing my neck before parking his chin on my shoulder.

Smiling brightly, I turned around in his arms. "Great game."

"Thanks."

"You hit a home run," I said, like maybe he hadn't realized it.

"I know it seems odd, considering how long I've played baseball, but I've never hit one before," he said. "But I knew, I knew as soon as I felt the bat make contact with the ball, that it was going to go out of the park. I don't know if it sounded different or felt different, but I just knew."

"You did look stunned out there."

"I was. Like I said, I'd never done that before. I mean, hitting has never been my strength."

"It was tonight." I reached up and kissed his chin.

"I need to figure out what it was I did that made me hit the home run."

"You connected the bat to the ball."

"No, it was more than that. Something I did before the game, maybe—"

"No, no, no," I said, lifting myself up onto my toes so I could look directly into his eyes. "There was no *thing* you did other than keeping your eye on the ball and hitting at the precise moment when the impact would send the ball over the fence."

"I'm not so sure."

"Okay, you want to know what it was? It was having me for a girlfriend—"

He put his hand behind my head and kissed me to shut me up. Obviously, he didn't think I understood the whole ritual scene, and in truth, I didn't.

I mean, sure, when I played softball, I always chewed cinnamon-flavored gum during the game, and I never started chewing until after the national anthem. But that was different. If I didn't do that, I missed way more balls than I caught.

But home runs? There was nothing that guaranteed home runs.

Jason drew back. "Maybe it *is* having

you for a girlfriend."

"I was kidding."

"I'm not. I like you a lot, Dani, but collegiate season ends in a few more weeks. I can't stay."

"I know."

"But I could come back . . . to visit."

I snuggled up against him. "That'd be great. And I'll come visit you."

"All right, folks, we're going to douse the lights," the announcer said.

The stadium went black. A colorful array of fireworks—green, yellow, white—burst into the air. A couple of seconds later, a boom sounded.

Everyone *oohed* and *ahhed*.

Even me. I'm a sucker for fireworks.

Jason pulled me closer, and everything I felt for him just seem to swell like those fireworks. It was glorious. Brighter than I'd expected it to be. Bursting forth with all sorts of emotions. Joy because he was mine. Sadness because he would be leaving. A scariness because I didn't know exactly what the future would hold for us.

Red, white, and blue streamers exploded against the black sky. The air popped.

I'd hoped for a summer boyfriend. Pick a boy. Any boy. How dumb was that?

But somehow I'd lucked out. When it came to boyfriends, I'd somehow managed to hit a home run. I was crazy about Jason. And he was crazy about me. And somehow, we'd make it work.

Another explosion of fireworks filled the sky. The colors faded away and then . . . a burst of red, *bang*, a burst of white, *bang*, a burst of blue, *bang*.

I was sure more followed, because I could hear the distant booms, but I was no longer watching the fireworks.

Jason was kissing me, and we were creating our own.

Turn the page for more summer romance!

So Inn Love

By Catherine Clark

Liza has finally landed her dream job, living and working at a beautiful beach resort on the coast of Rhode Island. Now she just needs to figure out how to be part of the in (inn) crowd—and whether her hot coworker Hayden could be more than just a summer fling.

Mediterranean Holiday

By Kate Cann

A summer on her own, a home on a tiny island off the coast of Malta, a cute boy-next-door—miles from home—could Chloe's holiday get any better?

So Inn Love

"Well, see you around, Beth," Caroline interrupted me. Then she turned back to the group she'd been talking to when I first walked up, to Zoe and her other friends.

Wow, I thought. If Caroline was part of the "in crowd," then maybe I didn't want to be. "It's Liza," I said to her back.

"Hey, Liza. And don't mind her, she's not that nice to anyone."

I turned and saw Hayden—the guy who'd arrived right after me—standing beside me. "Seriously?"

He nodded. "Caroline's not exactly the person you send out on the welcome wagon."

"Okay, but here's the thing. Have you ever seen a welcome wagon? Like, what's in it?"

"And who pulls it? Horses?" Claire added.

We all laughed, that kind of nervous laughter when you first meet someone.

"So you're Liza. And you are?" Hayden asked.

"Claire."

"So have I seen you here before?" he asked.

"No, we're new hires," Claire explained.

"You know, apparently the only two new people here?" I asked.

"Oh, come on, you're not the only new ones," Hayden said. "That guy Josh, over there . . . and that other guy, what's his name. There's at least five or six of you."

"Someone over there just called us new-bies," Claire said. "I hate that phrase, or term, or whatever it is."

"I know," I said. "It's like excuse us, we can't help it if we didn't work here before, but, you know, we didn't."

"So, non-newbies," Hayden said. "Don't get a complex. Hayden Overton. Nice to meet you."

"Same here," I said. At least one person in the so-called in crowd was being nice to us.

"You know what? You want to get out of here?" Hayden said.

"Aren't we supposed to go to the dorm?" Claire asked.

"The dorm can wait. Believe me," Hayden said. "Especially since —" He stopped and looked at us for a second.

"Since what?" I wanted to know.

He shook his head. "Never mind. We've got half an hour. Come on, let's hit the water."

I looked at Claire. "I'm all for it. You?"

"Sure," Claire said. "Sounds good."

"You know what—I see someone I've got to say hi to. But I'll be right down, okay?"

"He seems nice," Claire said as we walked outside onto the Inn's back porch, which stretched almost the entire length of the building. It had tables and chairs for guests, and standing on it, we looked straight out at the Atlantic Ocean.

"Very," I agreed. I stood on the steps for a few seconds, admiring the view. Then I stepped off onto the boardwalk and turned to look back up at the Inn. It was as gorgeous as I remembered. It was four stories tall, with white shutters and weatherbeaten-looking blue-gray paint. Every room had two windows, and a few of them had small decks with big Adirondack chairs facing the ocean.

"A private beach? This is incredible," Claire said as we stepped off the wooden boardwalk.

I slipped off my sneakers before I jumped off into the warm sand. Since the Inn wasn't open for business yet, the beach was all ours. "I've never been on this part of the beach."

I heard voices behind us and turned to see that everyone else had the same idea. Everyone was either walking—or sprinting—down to the ocean's edge like us, ditching their shoes, and sticking their toes into the ocean.

Suddenly I felt someone's hands on my shoulders.

"Are you ready for your initiation, newbies?"

I turned around and saw Hayden standing behind me. He squeezed my shoulders. "Initiation?" I asked. What was he talking about? This didn't sound good. And here I'd thought he was being so nice to us. "What's that?"

"It's a rite of passage," a guy named Richard said as he swooped up Claire in his arms, with one quick motion.

"Hey! Miss Crossley never mentioned this," Claire said. "Put me down!" she protested.

"You're not actually going to—" I started to say, as I struggled against Hayden. "You're not serious. You think you can—"

"Yeah, I do." He picked me up by the waist, sideways, like I was a suitcase under his arm, and dragged me closer to the water.

"Since when is there initiation around here?" Claire demanded.

"Since now!" And Richard lifted her in the air and tossed her into the surf.

Before I could laugh at her, I found myself being lifted over Hayden's head—and the next thing I knew I was underwater. It was freezing cold and bubbling up all around me as a wave tumbled over my head. My feet were standing on sand and crushed shells.

I stood up, surfaced, slicked back my hair, the salt water stinging my eyes.

Hayden was smiling at me as I strode out of the surf. "You actually liked that, didn't you?"

I pulled a piece of seaweed off my leg and threw it at him as I walked past. "Doesn't everyone like swimming?" I asked him with a smile.

Mediterranean Holiday

I got on the plane, almost literally beside myself with excitement. Davinia's parents had booked themselves into first class; we were in tourist.

But the great thing about it was, it was like we were traveling alone.

Davinia sauntered down the narrow aisle with me following and it was like her glamour and gorgeousness was flowing back on to me, making me that way too. I tried to copy her laid-back style despite being about to combust with excitement.

She was so elegantly calm and cool about everything. As we subsided into our seats (naturally, she took the window seat) I hissed, "Aren't you even the slightest bit excited?"

"You don't have to whisper, Chlo. It's not a frigging church. And yeah—course I am." Then she opened her magazine with a sigh.

I settled back, to enjoy being excited all on my own. To my left, a troop of lads was pushing by, all loud and swaggery and macho, the way boys do when they're in new territory together. As the fourth one walked by me the troop halted, and I looked past at the fifth boy.

He was perfect.

I wanted him.

I looked down, fast. He didn't move. Someone up ahead was taking a huge amount of time stowing their luggage. Thank you, someone! I started to take the boy in bit by bit. I slid sly looks at his legs, jean-clad, long, muscle-defined.

My eyes moved up to his crotch and screeched past, panic-stricken. I tipped my head back just a bit, looked at his arms, chest. Beautiful. My eyes glided upward, reached his face again.

He was looking right at me, like he was waiting for my eyes to get to his. He was gorgeous and grinning, all sarcastic and knowing.

I went red. Hideously red. Like a boiler suddenly being turned full on.

"Seen enough?" he drawled, all cock-sure.

I looked away, didn't answer. I hated him. And then the line moved on, and he went past.

I turned my head on the back of the seat,

straining my ears to hear what the boys were saying. All I could hear was this kind of happy rumbling, broken up regularly by the F word and jeering laughter. They sounded like they were having a lot better time than we were.

The man in the row behind us turned round bravely to the boys and asked them to keep their noise down. This was met with loud indignation and then I heard a voice say, "No, you're right, mate. We'll keep it down."

And the noise level dropped.

I still hated him, but somehow I wanted it to be him who'd said that, who had that kind of maturity, who commanded the respect of the others.

Clearly, I was slipping into a deep and obsessive psychotic state. Davinia, if she found out—which I'd make damn sure she never did—would be appalled.

Lunch arrived, in a whole set of fiddly plastic boxes, then cleared. Davinia didn't want to chat much. This would've bothered me before, but now I was so preoccupied I hardly noticed. I was not only preoccupied with the boy two rows back, I also needed—badly—to go to the toilet.

I nudged Davinia. "Shall we go to the loo?"

"What's the point of going together?" She yawned. "It just lengthens the queue."

I got unsteadily to my feet, and lurched along the tiny gangway. I could feel six pairs of male eyes on me, three pairs on each side. *Let me not trip up and land across their laps.*

I'd only been waiting in line a moment or so when I sensed someone draw up behind me. Close behind me. I thought it was Davinia changing her mind and then the next split instant I knew it wasn't and I had this overpowering, overwhelming sense that it was him. *Hurry up!* I screamed silently at the people ahead of me. *Calm down!* I screamed to myself.

I turned.

"All right?" he smirked. Face about a millimeter from mine, breathing god-breath all over me. Body right up against me, smell of cotton and male cologne. "Sorry," he said. "Bit of a crush, innit."

I thought I was going to die right there and then of adoration and desire. And then . . . THEN . . . "The bog's free," he announced, nodding toward the door swinging open again.

Then he grinned suggestively. "Unless you'd rather stay here, of course."

I waited inside the nasty toilet cubicle for absolutely sodding hours. I didn't care if they thought I had chronic diarrhea, I didn't care what they thought. Nothing could be as embarrassing as bumping into that jerk again. Twice—TWICE!—he'd made out I was lusting after him.

How dare he. I loathed him.